A Shot in the Dark . . .

He was thinking about Honey while he walked. If only the girl had known more. What she did know, what she told him, was just enough to raise his hackles, just enough to let him know that something about Ben Cranston and his death did not ring true.

He was about to pass by the Mexican's raucous and rowdy saloon when something so small he did not consciously recognize gave him the feeling that the skin on the back of his neck was drawing tight.

Longarm's gut clenched and his mouth became dry.

He stopped. Whirled. Dropped into a crouch, his double-action .45 in hand, eyes searching the shadows.

A lead-tipped spear of bright fire shot out from beside the flimsy building and a bullet's flight sizzled past his left shoulder.

If he had not stopped when he did . . .

Longarm took time to thumb back the hammer of his Colt. A simple squeeze of the trigger would do that job for him but the pistol was steadier, the trigger pull lighter, if the hammer was cocked manually. At a distance his aim held truer that way.

He saw a shadow shift slightly, and another flare of burning gunpowder came from the spot beside the saloon . . .

TABOR EVANS

LONGARM

AND THE COLD CASE

JOVE BOOKS, NEW YORK

THE BERKLEY PUBLISHING GROUP
Published by the Penguin Group
Penguin Group (USA) Inc.
375 Hudson Street, New York, New York 10014, USA
Penguin Group (Canada), 90 Eglinton Avenue East, Suite 700, Toronto, Ontario M4P 2Y3, Canada
(a division of Pearson Penguin Canada Inc.)
Penguin Books Ltd., 80 Strand, London WC2R 0RL, England
Penguin Group Ireland, 25 St. Stephen's Green, Dublin 2, Ireland (a division of Penguin Books Ltd.)
Penguin Group (Australia), 250 Camberwell Road, Camberwell, Victoria 3124, Australia
(a division of Pearson Australia Group Pty. Ltd.)
Penguin Books India Pvt. Ltd., 11 Community Centre, Panchsheel Park, New Delhi—110 017, India
Penguin Group (NZ), 67 Apollo Drive, Rosedale, Auckland 0632, New Zealand
(a division of Pearson New Zealand Ltd.)
Penguin Books (South Africa) (Pty.) Ltd., 24 Sturdee Avenue, Rosebank, Johannesburg 2196,
South Africa

Penguin Books Ltd., Registered Offices: 80 Strand, London WC2R 0RL, England

This is a work of fiction. Names, characters, places, and incidents either are the product of the author's imagination or are used fictitiously, and any resemblance to actual persons, living or dead, business establishments, events, or locales is entirely coincidental.

LONGARM AND THE COLD CASE

A Jove Book / published by arrangement with the author

PRINTING HISTORY
Jove edition / July 2011

ISBN: 978-0-515-14962-3

JOVE®
Jove Books are published by The Berkley Publishing Group,
a division of Penguin Group (USA) Inc.,
375 Hudson Street, New York, New York 10014.
JOVE® is a registered trademark of Penguin Group (USA) Inc.
The "J" design is a trademark of Penguin Group (USA) Inc.

PRINTED IN THE UNITED STATES OF AMERICA

10 9 8 7 6 5 4 3 2 1

Chapter 1

"I do like a man with a big . . ." She smiled and added, "Gun."

Custis Long stopped and stiffened—in more than one way—then returned the lady's smile.

She did seem to be interested, he thought, although he found it difficult to understand why she should be. The man generally known as Longarm did not consider himself to be handsome. Rugged, perhaps, with his sun- and wind-creased features. But not handsome.

The woman on the other hand was, um, toothsome to say the least. Probably on the sunny side of thirty. Red hair, green eyes, and dimples. Slender as a reed except for a most interesting swell of breast. But modest. Her clothes were impeccable, buttoned to the throat, sleeves down to her wrists.

"You are the United States marshal, aren't you?" she asked.

"Yes, ma'am, I have that honor."

"You should show me your . . . badge." Again that pause. That impish smile. "Sometime."

"Yes," he said, smiling back at her. "Sometime."

"Sometime," she said, making that sound more like a promise than a mere pleasantry. Then she turned quickly away, her skirts swirling out wide enough to brush Longarm's boots, and walked off at a brisk pace.

No nonsense in that one, Longarm told himself. He wondered who the hell she was. And how she might know that there was a deputy marshal in the neighborhood. Those were questions he intended to have answered. But not right now.

Longarm strode off in the opposite direction, a tall man in shades of brown. Brown flat-crowned Stetson. Brown tweed coat. Brown corduroy trousers. Tan calfskin vest. Brown-and-white-checked shirt worn with a string tie. Even his hair and handlebar mustache were seal brown.

But he was not quite entirely in brown. His gun belt and holster, worn for a cross draw, were polished black, as were his knee-high cavalry boots.

He was still wondering how the hell that redhead knew who he was. He'd only arrived in Bennett, Colorado, in the wee hours of the morning on the overnight coach from Hartsel down to Canon City and Pueblo. He had a quick drink at a friendly saloon and there was directed to a boardinghouse on the edge of the tiny mountain community.

That could explain it, he thought. The gent who ran the boardinghouse could have a wife—or a mistress for that matter—who told the redhead. The late-night bartender? He doubted it. Red showed more class than that. But some-damn-how she learned it. She was . . . mm, mighty interesting. Interesting enough to give him a hard-on just by the way she licked her lips when she looked at him.

Those lips looked soft and full and inviting. Just right for wrapping warm and wet around a man's cock. Just right for . . . Longarm shook himself, literally, and forced Red out of his thoughts. He was here on business. Serious business. He needed to pay attention to that.

He reached the end of the board sidewalk and paused to pluck a cheroot out of his inside coat pocket, nip the twist off with his teeth, and spit the bit of tobacco into the street. He extracted a sulfur-tipped match from his side pocket, where his supply lay mingled with his spare cartridges, and flicked the match into flame before he looked around—a man never knew where dangers might lie— and dipped his head to bring flame and cigar tip satisfyingly together.

"Damn, that tastes good," he muttered aloud when he drew the smoke deep into his lungs.

He looked around again, saw the place he sought at the end of the next block, and stepped down into the rutted street.

And jumped back again as a pair of horses came thundering out of an alley mouth and into the street, the horses running full out with necks extended and ears laid flat. On their backs were a pair of smallish riders with their bodies lying flat to the horses' necks and for all Longarm knew with their ears pinned back as well; that he could not actually see, for the pair were on him and past practically before a man could blink.

"Shit," he grumbled aloud. "Little bastards."

Behind him, Longarm heard a low chuckle. He turned to see an elderly man with a pure white mustache and side-whiskers, those presumably making up for the fact that he otherwise had no hair at all.

"Did you say something?" Longarm asked.

The gentleman, who was wearing a leather apron over a workingman's rough clothing, stepped forward and offered his hand. "I'm Titus Bennett," he said, "and I believe you would be the marshal."

"Deputy," Longarm corrected, shaking Bennett's hand. "Custis Long is the name." He glanced down the street in the direction where the two youngsters disappeared. "Does this sort of thing happen often?"

Bennett shrugged, then said, "Too often. You just met the Thomas twins. Their daddy owns the biggest mining operation around here. Most miners in this district are small potatoes. Work their own claims, maybe with a partner or two. Clete Thomas employs two dozen men to work his claims. Around here that makes him the big fish."

"So the little bastards can get away with terrorizing the community?"

"That is about the size of it," Bennett agreed.

"What about the local law?" Longarm asked. "I'm not asking about the Thomas boys. I need to see him about something else."

"First off," Bennett said, "they aren't Thomas 'boys.' They're Thomas girls, Betsy and Abigail. And don't ask me to tell you which was which. I've known them since they were waist high and I still can't tell them apart. Individually they're a handful. Together they're a full-blown terror.

"As for our local law, we don't have any. That's why we asked the marshal to send help up here."

Longarm grunted. "You know about that, do you?"

"Of course. Everyone does. Besides, I sit on the town council. We're the ones who wrote the letter."

"Mind if I ask you something, Mr. Bennett?"

Bennett smiled. "I can guess what the question will be and the answer is yes. I'm the self-aggrandizing old fart who named the town after himself. I made the initial claim and sold off parcels to those who came after. I'm no miner, though. I'm a cobbler. I used part of the money I received from selling the claims to open my shop here and to start a few other businesses. I suppose it would be fair to say that if Clete Thomas doesn't own it, I do."

"But I was told to see the man at the hardware and mining supplies store," Longarm said.

"That would be right. Jim Tanzy is our mayor. He's the one who officially signed the letter requesting you be sent here."

"Because of the Cranston gang," Longarm added.

Bennett nodded again. "We've heard threats that they intend to hoorah the town. Rob all the cash any of us has and burn all the buildings."

Longarm finished his smoke and flicked the butt into the street. "Why would a bunch like the Cranstons come all the way up here t' do a thing like that?"

"Because a few months ago, back before the weather broke, the youngest Cranston boy . . . named Billy or Bobby or whatever . . . got drunk in Bud Walker's saloon. He was loud and making a nuisance of himself, so Bud tossed him out the back door. Apparently the kid passed out in the alley or decided on his own to lie down and go to sleep. For whatever reason, he lay out there all night. He was dead . . . froze to death, we suppose . . . when

Bud found him in the morning. The Cranstons took umbrage to this. They want revenge. We're working people up here, Marshal. We aren't fighters. We certainly aren't gunmen. If the Cranstons want to tree our town, well, there won't be much we can do about it."

"Which is where I come in," Longarm said.

"Exactly," Bennett agreed. The old man sighed. "We need you here, Marshal. The fate of this entire community is riding on your shoulders."

Longarm grinned. "Not to put any pressure on me or anything."

"The good news is that anything you need, anything at all, all you need do is ask. We are all of us solidly behind you."

"That much is to the good," Longarm said. He took a deep breath, then said, "Thanks for the information, Mr. Bennett. Now if you'll excuse me, I need t' go make that courtesy call on your mayor."

"If you need anything, Marshal . . ."

"I'll ask," Longarm said. He touched the brim of his Stetson in salute to the old gentleman, stepped down into the street—there were no racing horses to dodge this time—and continued his journey to Tanzy's Hardware.

Chapter 2

"God, we're glad you're here to help us, Marshal," Tanzy said, wringing his hands nervously.

Jim Tanzy was a slight, bespectacled man. He reminded Longarm of Henry, clerk and secretary to Chief U.S. Marshal Billy Vail, Longarm's boss, at least outwardly. Tanzy looked like a good fart would knock him off his feet. But then so did Henry, and Henry's actions belied that frail appearance. Perhaps Tanzy would prove to be as solid a man as Henry was. Longarm rather hoped so, for if the entire Cranston gang showed up, he would be needing all the help he could get to put them in irons. Or to put them underground.

"I ran into Mr. Bennett on the way over here," Longarm told the mayor. "He explained a little o' what's going on. Why you're needin' help."

"Have you heard anything about the gang or when they might get here?" Tanzy asked.

Longarm shook his head. "No, sir. Far as I know, the

marshal hasn't got any word about their movements. We made out that if he does hear anything, he'll send a wire informin' me about it."

"Oh, we don't have the telegraph here, Marshal. I suppose we should but we don't. The nearest wires are up in Hartsel, and that key isn't manned full time. It is such a long way down to the Arkansas from here and the wires that run along it. To the north the telegraph runs through Florissant and Hartsel to Fairplay and then down to Buena Vista. It reaches the Arkansas there. Western Union says it just wouldn't pay to run wire all the way from Hartsel to Texas Creek just for our one little town. Bennett is the only community between Hartsel and the Arkansas, you see. If we need any wires sent, we take the coach up to Hartsel to handle it. I hope . . . I hope that won't ruin any plans you've made."

Longarm shook his head. "No plans, really. The boss knows where I am. If he needs t' get hold of me, he'll find a way, I'm sure."

"I certainly hope so. I . . . that is, we . . . are terribly concerned about the Cranstons. You know. What they could do to us. They say . . ." The man visibly shuddered at whatever dire thoughts he was having.

"That's why I'm here," Longarm said. Which was a bit of a stretch. The United States government did not officially give a shit about what did or did not happen to Bennett, Colorado. But it did care very much what happened to John, Louis, and Albert Cranston.

The trio of brothers, along with whatever collection of ruffians might be riding with them at any given moment, were wanted on outstanding warrants resulting from a robbery down in New Mexico Territory several years earlier. The brothers raided a stagecoach station and stole, among other things, a pouch containing mail.

During that robbery the Cranstons hoorahed the stage line employees, took cash and valuables from the passengers who happened to be there at the time, and when they were done, burned the stage station buildings.

That performance suggested that the rumors were probably accurate as to what the gang intended to do here in Bennett.

Longarm had also heard—it was not mentioned in the Wanted fliers, of course—that members of the gang terrorized and raped two women who happened to be passing through that stage station, along with a Mexican cook who was employed there.

Rape was a crime Longarm could not countenance.

He loved a good roll in the hay himself, but that was something that should be offered, not stolen. Freely offered or in exchange for cash, that was the woman's choice.

He thought it a great pity that rape was not a crime in the Federal statutes and so was not a matter he could enforce. Not, at least, officially.

That said, one could make a case that a man would be better off tried and convicted of the crime than to piss off Custis Long.

"Are you comfortable staying at Jennings's place?" Tanzy asked now.

Longarm smiled. "I'm a man who's used to boardinghouses, Mayor. After a spell they all seem the same. This one is about as good as any."

"Good. Good. Now if there is anything you need . . ." Tanzy let his voice trail off.

Longarm's smile flicked on and off again. "I'll let you know. Thanks. There is one thing you could do for me though."

"Anything. Just name it."

"This saloon where the Cranston boy froze t' death. Which one would that be?"

Tanzy gave directions, then hurried away to wait on a customer. Longarm ambled outside and down the street, back toward the same saloon where he had had a drink when he got off the coach during the night.

Chapter 3

"You'd be Bud Walker?" Longarm asked the gent wearing a more or less clean white apron.

"No," the bartender said, "but if it's important, I can get him for you."

"I'd 'preciate that, neighbor."

The bartender wadded up his towel and tossed it onto the bar, then disappeared into a back room. When he emerged a few moments later, he said, "Bud will be with you in a minute. Can I get you something while you're waiting?"

It was a little too early in the day for the rye whiskey that Longarm favored—assuming they had a decent label on hand in this out-of-the-way burg—but a beer and a handful of peanuts wouldn't go down bad. He gave his order, watched while the barman carefully drew one with only a minimal head on it, and munched a few peanuts out of the bowl on the bar. The beer was crisp and fresh and tasted just fine at any time of the day.

Longarm was halfway down in the schooner of pils-
ner when a portly gentleman wearing a red-and-black-
checkered flannel shirt came out. A thick patch of dark,
curly hair showed at his throat, matched by an unkempt
haystack of the stuff on top of his head. He must have
been clean shaven within the past week, but now his
jowls were dark with stubble. The fellow gave the appearance of a lumberjack whose muscle had gone to
seed. Or in this case to flab. Even so, he looked like
he would have been formidable in an arm-wrestling
contest. He stopped beside Longarm and extended his
hand.

"I'm Walker," he said. "You must be the deputy marshal. I have to tell you, Marshal, we were hoping for a
whole squad of you. There must be half a dozen or more
of the Cranstons."

Longarm introduced himself and added, "I'll do the
best I can t' keep your town from bein' killed off and
you folks with it."

Walker nodded, then said, "What can I do for you, Marshal?" Before Longarm had time to answer, Walker turned
to his barman and said, "Ted, Marshal Long here can't
pay for anything. Whatever he wants, it's on the house.
That's for as long as he is here, mind you."

"I hear you, boss," Ted said without interrupting the
busywork of washing mugs and shot glasses in a basin
of soapy water.

Walker turned his attention back to Longarm. "Well?"

"I'm wantin' to ask about Billy Cranston," Longarm
said.

"There isn't all that much to tell," Walker said with a
shrug. "He came in late of a winter's night. It was snow-

ing just a little, popcorn snow it was, and cold as a well digger's balls. The kid didn't say all that much at first, but he laid coin down and drank like he was starving for the stuff. Poured down straight shots, one atop another until he was knee-walking drunk, and the drunker he got, the louder he became. He was babbling about one notch below a shout, bragging about something or other. I didn't pay him much mind, really, except to be annoyed by the little bastard." Walker shifted his attention again and asked, "Ted, did you pay any mind to what that Cranston kid was growling about?"

Ted shook his head. "Not really. Something about what a big man he was and he could lick any man in the place, fists or knives or pistols, any one of them. That would've been the day. The little prick could hardly stand upright, much less tangle with a grown man. Or any half-grown one, for that matter."

Walker shrugged. "Bottom line, Marshal, he got to be pretty annoying. Some of the other customers, fellows from around here who are my bread and butter, they got to complaining. A couple of my regulars quit for the night and went home, and more started to fidget. I figured it was best that the boy leave. Told him so, but he just cussed and said he wouldn't. That's when me and Ted put him out the back door."

"Why the back door if you don't mind me asking?" Longarm said.

Walker laughed. "The kid was staggering around with his knees glued tight together and half bent over so it was pretty plain that he needed to take a piss. I figured he was either going to find the backhouse or he'd piss in his britches. That's why I put him out back."

Longarm chuckled. "Reckon I might've done the same thing then, Mr. Walker."

"Whoa now. Ted, is there anyone in this place with the first name of 'Mister'?"

"Not that I know of, Bud," the barman answered.

Walker looked back at Longarm and winked. "What else do you want to know, Marshal?"

"No one beat the kid or shot him or any such?"

"No, we just put him out back. Figured he could take his leak in the backhouse and then find his horse or whatever he wanted to do. I was surprised as anybody when he was found frozen stiff in the alley that next morning."

"What did you do with him then?"

"Everybody in town took a look at him. No one admitted to knowing who he was, although someone must have or the Cranstons wouldn't have been told what happened to him. We had the viewing, like I said, then we took him up the hill yonder"—he tilted his head toward the back wall of the saloon—"and gave him a decent burial. At town expense, I might add. The ground was frozen solid for two feet down so we had to use three quarter-sticks of dynamite to open the grave. I paid for that out of my own pocket, him having been a customer even if it was for only the one night."

"I'd say the town of Bennett did right by Billy Cranston," Longarm observed.

"Tell that to the Cranston gang when they get here."

"I expect to," Longarm said, reaching for a cheroot.

"Don't light that," Walker quickly said. "Ted, get the marshal a cigar. One of those Hernandez y Hernandez pales. And some matches."

"Coming right up."

Good beer and now a plump Hernandez y Hernandez pale leaf cigar? Longarm wouldn't mind if the Cranston boys took their sweet time about coming to hoorah Bennett.

He saluted Bud Walker with the freshly lighted smoke, hooked a boot onto the brass rail that ran along the front of the bar, and considered himself mighty comfortable, mighty fortunate. This was the kind of assignment he could enjoy.

Chapter 4

Longarm stifled a yawn and pushed his empty mug aside.

"Another?" the barman offered. Longarm shook his head.

"No thanks, Ted. You overheard what I was talkin' to your boss about, I suppose."

"Sure I did," the bartender said, laying his towel down and tugging at the edges to straighten it out.

"D'you know anything more about this boy Billy Cranston?"

"No, I don't. I never paid him any particular mind until he got so loud and annoying. Didn't know who he was and wouldn't have cared if I did know. He was alive and healthy when me and Bud took him out back. Drunk as a lord, of course, but loud. Singing and like that. I never in this world expected he would lay out there and freeze to death."

"Assuming that's what killed him," Longarm said.

"I sure don't know what else it could've been."

"But he wasn't examined by a doctor, right?"

"We got no doctor here, though we could sure use one. Accidents and all that, you know."

"Where's he buried?" Longarm asked.

"Our cemetery is over the hill just south of the string of businesses along the main street. If you want to see the boy's grave, it's the only one there without any marker of any sort. We covered it over with stones to keep the varmints out, but at the time we didn't have no name to put on it. Didn't know if he was a believer . . . though he didn't act like one if he was . . . so we didn't put a cross on it neither."

"All right, thanks."

Longarm dropped a nickel on the bar to pay for his beer. If Ted wanted to take that as a tip instead of allowing Longarm to pay his own way, well, that was up to him. Longarm tugged the brim of his hat down lower and ambled outside.

He crossed the street and walked through an alley to get to the open country that rimmed the little mining town. A narrow path angled from east to west up the slope of the low hill that lay just south of Bennett. The creek that was the focus of the mining claims ran east of town. The camp had advanced far beyond the panning stages of gold recovery. Now most were operating rockers. The one large outfit was to the northeast. That would be Clete Thomas's mine burrowing into a hill on the other side of the creek.

Longarm paused to light a cheroot, then took the path that led over the hill to the cemetery.

The soil was gravel and red clay, the grasses sparse, dry and as much gray as green. There were only three grave mounds inside the scantling fence that surrounded the cemetery. Two of them were marked with slabs of stone inscribed with the names of men who were buried there. The third, at the edge of the enclosure, remained unmarked.

Longarm wondered if the Cranstons could be talked into properly honoring their brother with a stone instead of burning down the town where he died.

Probably not. But it might be worth a try if he could get them to talk, and think, rationally.

He did notice something a little odd when he looked at the grave. Someone, it seemed, had been tending the plot. Fresh, dark dirt showed where weeds had very recently been pulled on and near Billy Cranston's grave mound.

The soil was much too hard to take the impression of the shoes or boots of whoever it had been, although he looked anyway just to be sure.

Longarm turned away with a grunt, finished his cheroot, and tossed the butt down. There was no danger of starting a grass fire here, but habit prompted him to grind the stub of the slender cigar underfoot anyway.

He headed back to Bennett with even more questions now than he had when he walked up there.

Billy Cranston was said to know no one in Bennett. He was a stranger. Yet someone was tending to his grave. Longarm wondered who. And why.

It was nearing lunchtime now. He had been jawing all morning and his belly was growling. His room did not

come with a noontime meal, so he would have to find
another place where he could grab some grub.

Relief came in the form of an old Sibley tent, its canvas
ragged and sun bleached. A crudely lettered sign hanging from one of the guy lines said EATS.

The interior held two chest-high benches where the
diners could stand while they shoveled food into their
maws. The benches, situated so the diners stood facing
each other across a narrow alley, were long enough to
comfortably hold ten men at a time standing side by
side. When Longarm arrived, there were ten men at one
bench and eleven crowding the other. A harried-looking
young woman was kept busy moving up and down between the benches, refilling bowls of what smelled like a
purely delicious stew.

The cook, an older man with gray hair on his head
and wool enough on his arms and upper body that he
would have to watch himself come shearing time, was
doing his cooking over the biggest sheepherder's stove
Longarm had ever seen.

His larder was a single huge chest that rested on four
stones, the stones sitting in pans full of water, a device
that would keep ants away, while a closed lid on the trunk
should suffice to keep rats out overnight.

Another, smaller chest held pans, skillets, knives, and
the rest of the hardware necessary to run an eatery.

The best part of it, Longarm realized, was that everything there could be packed up in an afternoon's time
and put in the back of a buckboard for transport to the
next strike, however far that might be.

A few of the diners looked up at his entry but no one spoke. They were too busy stuffing themselves with stew and cornbread.

What the hell, Longarm figured. When in Rome and all that. He squeezed in at the end of the bench that held only ten.

"Twenty-five cents," was the greeting he got from the girl as she slammed an enameled steel bowl and a spoon down in front of him.

Longarm dug into his britches for the coin, which she dropped into her apron pocket. "Thank you, ma'am."

The girl was small. She might have been pretty, he thought, if she would wash the grease out of her hair and maybe scrub her face a little while she was at it. She had dark hair that straggled over her face, brown eyes, and a rather small mouth. Her chin was a little too weak for her to ever be considered a beauty, but even so, she was not an ugly little thing. He could not tell anything about her figure, thanks to the heavy canvas apron that covered her to her ankles. When she turned to fetch his stew, he saw that she was wearing miner's garb, denim trousers and a red-and-black-checked shirt.

"Thank you again," he said when she ladled a generous portion of stew into his bowl and pushed a platter of pan-fried corn pone to where he could reach it.

This time the girl glanced up for a brief moment. She even took time to smile. Then she was gone, serving up second helpings—or thirds, fourths, whatever—to the others ranked along the twin benches.

Longarm took a tentative bite of the stew. Then smiled. The old cook's son-of-a-bitch stew was about as good as he'd ever tasted. His next bite was considerably bigger. And the ones after that. And . . .

Bennett, Colorado, was proving to be not such a bad assignment after all. Now if only he could make that redhead's acquaintance.

Chapter 5

Longarm took his time with the stew and . . . with whatever the other might be called. It was about halfway between squaw bread and corn pone. Damn good whatever it was called. He stood at the bench and thoroughly enjoyed both, eating slowly and idly listening to the conversations that droned through the tent.

Along about his third bowl of stew—they likely would make him pay again if this kept up; not that it was much of a factor since his belly was about to burst already—something occurred to him. He let go of his bowl and spoon then and ducked out the back of the tent for a smoke while he killed some time.

He could see underneath the canvas, and when the last pairs of rubber boots disappeared and the men went back to their diggings, he returned to the rustic café.

The cook and the girl were up to their elbows in hot water and lye soap, cleaning the bowls and silverware from the lunch crowd. The girl saw his approach from the back of the place. She turned, hands dripping, and tossed the bowls she had been scrubbing into a washtub of more or less clean water.

"Yes, sir? Didn't you get enough lunch?"

Longarm grinned at her. "I'm full as a tick on a hound's ear, miss, but I thank you. I was, uh, wanting t' ask you about something else."

"Of course, Marshal. Everyone in Bennett wants to cooperate any way we can." She reached for a cloth to dry her hands on and said something to the cook in a language Longarm did not think he'd ever heard before.

He raised an eyebrow in inquiry and the girl said, "I told my father that I will speak with you. His English is not so good."

"What was that you talked to him in?"

"Turkish," the girl said. "We are from Turkey. In this country since I was little but my papa"—she shrugged—"he is trying to speak better."

"You don't have any accent hardly," he said. It was almost true. Her voice was more husky than accented. He liked it.

"Can we walk, please? It is a treat to be away from the restaurant in daybreak." She frowned, then corrected herself. "Daylight, that should be."

"Yes. Daylight. Anywhere you would like to walk?"

"Up the hill if you do not mind. I love the clean air here and the long views. The mountain peaks all around." She hugged herself, seemed to remember the heavy apron, then and with a flush of embarrassment glowing in her cheeks, took it off.

The girl hung the apron on a spike where a side support pole protruded through a grommet at the back of the tent.

"I'm Marshal Long, by the way," he said when she turned around again. He smiled. "Longarm to my friends."

"Then I hope I may call you Longarm. My name is Mariska Cook." She laughed at the puzzlement Longarm showed. She quickly explained. "The man when we enter this country, he does not know to . . . excuse me, know *how* to spell our name. So here in the United States of freedom our name is Cook. I do not know if this is because it is what my father does or because all names being given that day begin with *C*." Her laugh was soft and melodic and she shrugged again. "It is a good name, yes?"

"A very good name," he agreed, following Mariska away from the creek where the miners labored and cursed.

They ambled along through the grass and the weeds and the low-growing Indian paintbrush. On a whim Longarm bent and plucked one of the tender, scarlet blossoms and handed it to Mariska. Her answering smile was bright as a bull's-eye lantern, and she tucked the flower into her hair. It looked very nice there, and he told her so.

"Thank you. The men I see, they want to eat. Quick, quick. Then back to their gold. They do not give flowers to girls." She laughed. "In the camp there are girls they give their gold. I think those girls make more gold than the men do, what do you think?"

"I think you're right."

They reached a stand of young aspen. Mariska stopped and leaned back against a tree trunk. "You say you want to talk with me?"

"I do, Mariska. D'you mind if I smoke?"

"I do not mind."

He pulled a cheroot from inside his coat—the supply there was growing slim; soon he would have to find some more—and took his time lighting it. Mariska patiently waited. She seemed comfortable doing so.

"A little while ago I was noticin' that the men in your café talk pretty open. Pretty loud, too."

"Yes, many of them do," she agreed.

"I was wonderin' if you know anything about Billy Cranston, the boy that was killed, the one those brothers are so mad about."

"I do not know much," she said. "His name was not Billy. I know that much. He was Benny. Benjamin Cranston. He was not a criminal. This, too, I know."

"An' how would you be knowin' this?" Longarm asked.

Mariska shrugged. "Like you say. I hear things."

"Some things you'd rather not pass along, is that it? Or where you heard them?"

Another shrug.

"D'you happen t' know who's been tending to Ben Cranston's grave?"

"Is this important?"

"Is it you?" he countered.

"No, Marshal, is not me."

"But you know who it is," he said. It was not really a question.

"Is not for me to say. Please understand."

"You promised not t' say anything?" he guessed.

The girl did not answer.

"I know that a promise is meant t' be kept," Longarm

told her, "but if it looks like the safety o' this whole town is at stake, I'll ask you again. An' tell you that it's important. If I do that, Mariska, I'll expect you t' answer, promise or no promise. D'you understand?"

She paused, then slowly nodded. "Yes. I understand this, Marshal."

"Longarm," he said with his most boyishly disarming smile.

Mariska's answering smile was sweet and innocent.

On an impulse he said, "Are you doin' anything this evening after supper?"

"Oh, Longarm, there is nothing in Bennett to do after dark. Only if you drink or visit the bad women."

"I was thinkin' it might be nice to walk out with you in the night air. Once you get away from the camp, the pines smell awful nice. We could just set and . . . you know. Talk."

"I would like that. My papa closes the tent as soon as it is dark." She laughed. "The men, they do not know why but I tell you. It is because he is too cheap to buy oil for the lamps. So the men all know if they want to eat, they come early. They can drink later but eat before dark. Give me time to help Papa with the washing up. Then I would . . . I would be happy to walk with you."

Longarm smiled and gave her a little bow. "Honored, ma'am."

Mariska surprised him by dropping into a curtsy. She pulled it off rather well considering that she was wearing pants instead of a skirt.

Without another word, the girl turned and hurried back to the café tent, where he supposed she and her father would be busy getting supper ready for the evening crowd.

Chapter 6

Longarm had not seen any whores in Bennett, but what Mariska said was a sure and certain indication that there were some. And whores, if you could get them to talk, could be a splendid source of information.

He had a clear sense that there was much more to Benjamin Cranston's death than he at first thought. Accident or not—and he had no reason to think otherwise—it was not a simple death. Someone who lived here in Bennett was tending to the young fellow's grave. That fact gnawed at his gut. Someone here felt . . . something . . . for Cranston. Someone who seemed to be hiding that fact. A lover? Quite possibly. It could be that that was the reason Cranston came here in the first place. A shattered romance and a broken heart that led to Ben Cranston's drinking binge that night? Damn near anything was possible.

The one thing Custis Long knew for sure was that he wanted to learn more.

Another thing he was sure of was that Mariska Cook knew more than she was willing to tell. Perhaps tonight he could convince her to break her promise and tell him what she knew.

But that would be tonight and this was still early in the afternoon.

Which reminded him. Sort of. He pulled the bulbous Ingersal watch from his vest pocket, found the key that was dangling from a slender chain along with the fob on that end of his watch chain—the other end being occupied by his derringer—and carefully wound the bulky but accurate railroad watch. It was, um, 2:17 precisely.

First things first, he thought, and Bennett's whores should be considered his first line of inquiry now that he knew there was more to be learned than he first thought.

He returned to the rutted street and followed it to the other end of town, away from Bud Walker's saloon, past another, and on to the edge of Bennett, where the shabbiest of the community's three saloons was located.

If this one had a name, it was not apparent. Very likely no one had bothered to name it, not even by the moniker of the fat, greasy Mexican proprietor who sat like a brown toad on a stool at one end of the bar.

The Mex looked up when Longarm entered but did not bother to reach for one of the tin mugs stacked close to hand, nor did he make any move toward the beer kegs or jugs of skullpop.

"You're that marshal man," the Mex said.

"I am," Longarm admitted. "Custis Long is my name."

"I know."

"You are . . . ?"

"Is not important, I think." The Mex shifted to the

other cheek of his more than ample ass. A moment later he leaned sideways and blew a resounding fart. He grunted. "Yeah. That is important, eh."

"I need t' find out more about this Cranston kid," Longarm said. "Was he in here the night he died?"

The Mex raised both hands, palm upward, and said, "That was months ago, no? Who can remember these things?"

"You can if you want to," Longarm suggested.

"I don' think so."

Short of beating something out of the man—and that might have no faint acquaintance with the truth—Longarm would seem to be at a dead end here.

"Give me a drink, huh? Whiskey."

"I don' got whiskey," the Mex said.

"Bullshit. I see those jugs setting there beside you."

"Water chaser for the beer."

"More bullshit." Longarm leaned across the split aspen plank that was serving as a bar and hefted one of the jugs. He pulled the cork, sniffed, then took a small sip. Very small. The stuff tasted like horse piss. Hell, it may have *been* horse piss. But with a hefty jolt of alcohol in it, too.

There was no question that it was homemade liquor. Therefore, no taxes had been paid on it. Therefore, he could arrest the Mexican on that charge. If he wanted to. He figured he would need a reason to want that. Like leverage to use against the man at some time in the future. If it seemed like a good idea come that time.

The Mex looked a little nervous—hell, he knew no Federal tax had been paid on his so-called whiskey quite as well as Longarm did—then considerably relieved when

Longarm pushed the cork back in place and set the jug back where he had gotten it.

Longarm laid a nickel on the bar and said, "Thanks for the drink. Now where can a man find a female companion?"

"Companion?"

"A woman to fuck," Longarm clarified. "Where can I get laid?"

"Oh, that. I don' got no puta here."

"Yeah, I see that, but where in this town can I find some?" Longarm persisted.

"Are you sure . . . ?"

"I need t' know."

"A'right. You go over by the creek, then upstream past Mr. Thomas's digging. There is a place . . . three, four cabins, like . . . placed in a group. You know? It is, oh, quarter mile past Mr. Thomas. You can't miss it."

Can't miss it. Longarm often wondered why the hell everyone said that. If he couldn't miss it, he wouldn't be asking, would he?

Or was he just feeling a little touchy for a reason or reasons he could not at the moment identify?

"Thanks," he told the Mexican and strode out of the place. Custis Long rarely met a saloon that he did not like, but he definitely did not care for this one.

He glanced toward the sun to make sure he had plenty of afternoon remaining before his "date" with Mariska Cook, then headed at a rapid pace toward Bennett's whorehouse.

Chapter 7

"We aren't open for business right now, mister. Come back after supper."

Longarm displayed his badge and the dark-haired girl with the mole on her cheek—probably artificial—opened up and let him in.

His presence brought the working girls out into the parlor, probably hoping to turn an early trick and get a head start on the night's earnings.

The house had six girls working, each one of them a cut above the usual run of mining camp whores. These would have scrubbed up good enough for polite society. At least they washed their makeup off periodically and brushed their hair. They ranged in height from here to there and in weight from skinny to huge.

"What can we do for you, Marshal?" asked the girl who opened the door to him.

"First off, I reckon I need t' see your madam."

"She isn't here right now. Can I take a message for her?"

Longarm helped himself to a seat on a wingback chair. A plump little blonde tried to slip onto his lap but he turned her aside. "Maybe you girls can help me," he said.

"Sure. If we can. Would you like a drink or something?"

"No, I . . . say, d'you have any rye whiskey?"

The girl smiled. "Only the best." She turned her head and said, "Bunny, go get the marshal some of that good stuff she keeps for Mr. Bennett."

A girl with henna red pigtails hurried out of the room. She was back moments later bearing a cut glass tumbler with two fingers of liquor in it. Longarm bent his head over the whiskey and inhaled. When he looked up, he smiled.

"Is that all right, Marshal?"

"Best I've had in many a moon," he said. It was almost true. He could find better in Denver but he had to search for it. He certainly would not have expected to find anything of this quality in an out-of-the-way place like Bennett.

He took a measured sip, held the whiskey on his tongue for a moment, and then swallowed. Finally he said, "I'm tryin' to learn more about Benny Cranston."

"He's the boy that froze to death this winter, right?"

Longarm nodded. He found it mildly interesting that the girls so readily accepted the name "Benny" while everyone else in town was calling the dead boy "Billy." He treated himself to another sip of the good rye. "I'm told he used to come here," he lied. No one had told him any such thing, but it seemed logical that a traveling youngster with money in his jeans might well have wanted to get his ashes hauled. And this was the place to handle that chore.

The girls looked back and forth to one another, then their collective gaze focused on Longarm. "No, sir. We heard about him, of course. Everyone around here has. But if he ever came here, we never knew which one he was," the girl with the mole said. "We never saw him, of course. Not after he was dead, I mean. And our gentleman callers don't generally give us their names."

A couple of the girls giggled, and the one with the mole added, "Not their real names anyhow."

"Are you sure?"

"No, sir, we're not at all sure. He could've come here, like I just told you, but we wouldn't have no way to know it was him."

"Maybe," another girl put in, "you could describe his pecker. That's all most of us looks at anyhow. We could tell you for certain if we knew what his prick looked like."

"How big," a big, busty mulatto explained, "or if he had moles on it or something."

"I haven't looked," Longarm said dryly, "but I'll keep your suggestion in mind."

"What about yours, Marshal? Can we get a look at yours? Do you have a big one? Which way does it lean? If you want one of us, you could have it for free."

"Or two of us," another said.

"I think you girls are getting carried away here," Longarm said, standing. "This would be a good time for me t' leave."

That brought more giggles from the girls. He tossed back the shot of rye, then thanked them and headed for the door, no better informed than when he came. Before he stepped outside, he paused and asked, "When will your boss be back?"

The dark-haired girl had followed him to the doorway while the others trooped toward the back of the place. "I would be glad to tell you, Marshal, but we never know. She comes and goes."

"All right, thanks. I'll check back with her later on sometime. Please tell her that I called. An' what it is I was wantin' here."

"I will, Marshal. That's a promise."

Longarm touched the brim of his Stetson and headed back toward town.

Chapter 8

Longarm was more than a little bit sorry that he'd passed up the offer of a free fuck. His pecker was telling him he should have stayed—it was not like he had anything better to do while he waited for the Cranstons to ride into town—but in this case professionalism won out over horniness. Reluctantly.

He walked back into town, glancing every now and then toward the hill where Ben Cranston was buried. There was something that puzzled him about the young fellow's death. Why had Cranston lain down in the alley and frozen to death there? If he had been on his feet when Bud Walker and Ted threw him out the back door, surely he should have been able to stagger to his horse.

Come to think of it, where had Cranston been staying in Bennett? There were not so many possibilities. He must have had lodging somewhere.

Scowling at the unanswered questions, Longarm headed for Titus Bennett's boot repair shop.

He found the old man bent over his cobbler's bench, hammer in hand and his mouth bristling with tiny copper nails. Bennett looked up at Longarm's arrival but did not speak until he first spit the nails into the palm of his hand.

"Good afternoon, Marshal. Is the town taking good care of you?"

"Very good, thank you, but I have a few questions if you don't mind."

"Anything at all, Marshal. You are our protection and we wouldn't want to do anything to distress you. Ask whatever you like."

Longarm tipped his Stetson back on his head, went behind the counter, and straddled a stool close to Bennett's workbench. "I'm curious about the dead boy, Titus. Was there a coroner's inquest held?"

"No, we have no coroner here. Nothing so official. The town itself is not organized or chartered. All of our offices are unofficial and the county takes no notice of us."

"Was he at least examined before he was buried?" Longarm asked.

Bennett shrugged. "Not as far as I know. Don't forget, at the time we had no idea he had any significance. He was a stranger passing through who lay down and froze to death. That was all we knew. Someone rolled him up in a blanket and sewed it closed for his shroud. There was no coffin. I helped open the grave myself and read over him. The grave was closed and we came back to town. And that was that. We all went back to tending to our own affairs and more or less forgot about the boy until we began to hear these rumors about his family coming to burn the town down around our ears."

"Did you see the body?"

Bennett shook his head. "The shroud was already closed when I got there. I don't know who did that. It was sewed with rawhide. Very ordinary stuff that you might find anywhere. The blanket"—the old man shrugged—"it might have been his own, taken from his horse or . . . I just don't know."

"Come to think of it," Longarm said, "what happened to that horse?"

"The horse and its rigging was sold for the cost of the burying. I believe Clete Thomas has it. Clete's girls have an eye for horses. As you learned for yourself this morning."

"Is it an especially good horse?"

"I wouldn't know," Bennett said. "I have little experience with horses and don't know them well. It looked like a nice enough horse, but I couldn't tell you beyond that."

"All right. Thanks, Titus." Longarm pulled out his watch and glanced at it. It was probably time he started back toward George Jennings's boardinghouse. He had already been warned that if he arrived late for a meal, he would be out of luck.

He saluted the old cobbler with a finger to his hat brim and left, walking swiftly. And thinking.

Among other things, he was still wondering why he was so reluctant to accept the story of Ben Cranston's death and quick burial. It was all perfectly logical and ordinary. Yet there was something . . .

Chapter 9

Longarm parted the fly beads that hung in the doorway of George Jennings's boardinghouse. Not that the beads seemed to do much good judging by the buzzing visitors that had joined them for supper.

The supper, on the other hand, had been a typically satisfying boardinghouse meal, plain and bland and long on quantity rather than quality. Breakfasts were generally porridge or mush, suppers rice and gravy along with a pan-fried meat of some kind. Tonight it had been lamb chops served one per customer. That was all right. Longarm had damn sure had worse.

Now his belly was full and his mood good. He went outside and chose one of the rocking chairs set there for the patrons of the house. There was no porch or wooden platform, just the rockers sitting on the hard, gravel-filled clay soil.

Two of his fellow boarders were loudly bragging about the quality of their claims. So loudly, in fact, that Longarm suspected they were trying to plant the idea that he would be better off if he bought the claims from one or both of them.

He was not so inclined.

He settled back on the rocker, plucked a cheroot from his coat pocket—the supply replenished from his carpet bag before supper—and snapped a match aflame to light it.

From the front of the boardinghouse he could see most of the town of Bennett.

Including, he noticed, that redhead he'd run into early in the morning. She came out of one storefront—a tailor if he remembered correctly—and walked toward the other end of town.

Longarm felt himself getting hard again. Professionalism or no, he would not have turned that one down this afternoon. Lordy, she was one fine-looking woman. And there was something about her, a presence or perhaps a scent, that suggested she was one very sexy female. He wanted her. Bad. If he hadn't already made plans to go walking with Mariska Cook, he might well have made a run at her. As it was, well, no. But he sure as hell thought about it.

From where he sat, he could see the tent café where Mariska and her father worked. No lights showed beneath the sides, and as dusk was turning into night, he could see the tent flaps lowered and secured in place, closing the café down for the night.

Longarm finished his cheroot, then stood and walked to the café.

"Mariska?" he called softly from outside the tent flap.

"Come to the back, please," she responded from the other side of the canvas.

He did, tripping over a guy rope only once in the process. Mariska stood behind the tent waiting for him.

There was enough light remaining in the sky for him to see that the girl had washed her face and brushed her hair, put on what was likely her very best dress—perhaps her only dress—and now she smelled of . . . it took him a moment to remember . . . vanilla extract, the poor girl's perfume. Longarm smiled. Mariska had gone to considerable trouble to make herself ready for this date.

The least he could do was to act the gentleman in appreciation. He bowed low then offered his arm. The girl placed her hand in the crook of his elbow and tossed her head. She smiled, looking the prettier for it.

"Shall we go back up the hill like this afternoon?" she asked.

Longarm shook his head. "Let's go the other direction. I haven't seen what's over there exactly, but I know there's some trees not too far. Maybe we can find some blowdown where we can set while we talk."

"Wherever you lead, Mr. Longarm, I will follow," she said. She was a pert little thing, more cute than pretty, but he liked her.

They walked in silence for a spell, passing between two crudely constructed buildings set along the main street, and on into a field of rabbit brush and wire grass. Beyond that was a stand of pine with a clump of pale aspen off to the right.

He saw no pine blowdown, but there was a sizable

aspen trunk that had been felled by wind or lightning. Longarm led the girl to it. "Will this be all right?"

"Perfect," she declared. She stood tall for a moment, breathing deeply. When she turned and settled onto the log, she said, "You were right. The pine scent in the air is fresh and clean and wonderful. Thank you for bringing me."

"My pleasure," he assured her. He took a seat on the log beside her, choosing to sit above Mariska on the slope of the downed tree. She was on his right. "Are you okay there?" he asked.

"Yes, I . . . no, I'm scared I might fall. Would you mind putting your arm . . . oh, yes, that is ever so much better."

A few moments later she said something about sliding. Which prompted a smile on his part because she was talking about sliding but . . . uphill?

The result of the so-called sliding was that she was pressing tighter and tighter against him.

Then somehow she became turned around so that she was facing him.

And her face—lovely in the moonlight—was lifted to his.

Longarm found himself kissing the girl, hardly knowing how or when it happened, although he was making no complaint.

She tasted of peppermint and some warm, heavier flavor. Peach brandy, perhaps.

Mariska made the first move, her tongue sliding deep into his mouth as she explored his lips and ran her tongue over his teeth.

She moaned softly and reached for his hand, lifting it

to her breast and placing it atop her right tit. She did not have much there, but what he found was soft and warm, her nipple hard against his palm.

He quickly unbuttoned the top of her dress and slipped his hand inside. Mariska moaned again as his fingers found and toyed with the taut flesh of her nipple.

Longarm turned and picked the girl up off the tree trunk, his mouth never leaving hers in the process. He carried her a few feet to a patch of sweet grass then bent and placed her down, settling beside her.

He lay the girl back and leaned over her, his tongue leaving her mouth to rove across her cheek and into her ear, back down onto her throat and then lower until he took her nipple into his mouth, swirling it around and around until Mariska moaned, her hips rotating and her pelvis thrusting insistently upward.

Longarm slid his hand underneath the hem of her dress. She was not wearing any drawers and he found that she was dripping wet, her juices slick and slippery. Ready to receive him.

By then she was fumbling at the buttons of his fly. He helped her and soon his cock sprang free, ready.

"Big," she whispered. "You are so big. I like big man."

Mariska grasped his prick tight and pulled, urging him on top of her. Into her.

He slipped easily into the well-lubricated entry to her. The heat of her small body enveloped him, and as he plunged deep inside the girl, he could feel her hipbones hard against his pelvis.

She took everything he had, constantly moaning and wriggling beneath him.

Longarm braced himself above her and let Mariska's writhing take over as she impaled herself on his pole time and time again.

Quickly the sensations built within his balls until all too soon his fluids burst deep into her body. He held himself still, poised inside her, until the last spasms of pleasure were sated and it became nearly painful to remain.

Mariska clutched him tight, her thin arms wrapped around him, and he remained locked inside the girl's body for long moments while her breathing and his returned to something approaching normal.

"You are . . ." he hoarsely groaned, "damn good."

The girl's response was a pleased sigh and placing her cheek against his sweaty chest.

"I'm . . . too heavy . . . atop you," he breathed.

She held him even tighter. "Stay. Please stay. Just a little longer. It feels so very good, you inside me like this."

"I'm not too heavy?"

"No. I like to feel you there." She clung like she never wanted to let him go, so he relaxed and let the girl take his weight onto her small body.

It amazed him sometimes what a woman's body was designed to accept. The smallest woman could accept a huge man that logic said would crush her, yet she not only could accept his weight, but could fuck his boots off while she did it.

"Hmm." He bent his head low and kissed her. "I like goin' on a walk with you."

He could feel himself growing hard again. Mariska could quite obviously feel it, too, as again she began to move her hips, slower this time and more gently as she guided them both to a another sweetly satisfying climax.

It was not until several very pleasant hours later that Longarm walked a fully dressed and indeed quite virginal-appearing Mariska back to her father's tent.

Chapter 10

Longarm bade Mariska good night with a chaste hand-shake in case anyone might be watching. He saw her inside the big tent, then wandered down the street to Walker's saloon.

The place was not exactly a beehive of activity, but there were eight or ten other gents enjoying beer or cheap whiskey. Longarm stood at the bar, where a group of three were quietly drinking and talking. A fourth man was by himself to Longarm's right.

"I'll have a beer, Ted."

"And one for me?" the fellow on his right said, sliding over close to Longarm's elbow.

"Don't you be bothering the marshal, Ford. You know better than that. You know Bud's rules. If you badger the paying guests, you won't be allowed in here anymore."

"I was just . . ."

"I know what you were just up to, Fargo. Now take the rest of that beer and haul your ass away from the man."

Longarm put a dime on the bar and said, "I can stand him one beer, Ted."

"Thank you. Thank you, Marshal." The man practically quivered with gratitude.

Longarm grunted a response and turned slightly away from Fargo. There was something about the man that made Longarm think he was more than a bit of a weasel.

The bartender saw Longarm's distaste and helped by setting Fargo's beer well down the bar, drawing him away from conversation with the tall lawman.

"Thanks," Longarm said with a wink when Ted set his beer in front of him. He lifted the mug and was about to take his first throat-cleansing swallow when a disheveled miner came rushing in the door, his chest heaving for breath.

"Is . . . is . . . marshal . . . where . . . oh, thank God. There you are." He ran to Longarm and clutched at his sleeve. "You got to . . . come . . . come quick . . . there's gonna be murder."

Longarm slammed his mug down and barked, "Where?"

"This . . . this way."

Longarm followed the fellow outside and down the street toward the Mexican's seedy saloon, Longarm's long legs quickly leaving the miner behind once he realized where they were headed.

He burst through the door with his Colt already in hand.

Inside the poorly lighted saloon he saw he was already too late to stop the violence. A man knelt on the sawdust-littered ground, bent over double holding his guts in his hands while another miner stood over him holding a foot-long Bowie, its blade marred with fresh blood.

"Drop the knife," Longarm ordered.

The dozen or so men in the place all turned to look at the lawman who'd suddenly appeared among them. All, that is, except the man on the ground, the one who was already as good as dead from the knife stroke.

"Drop . . . the . . . knife," Longarm repeated, slowly and forcefully.

The fellow with the Bowie looked down at his own knife, his eyes dull, his expression blank, as if he were somehow detached from what was taking place.

"Drop it," Longarm said again. He lifted his Colt and looked into the knife wielder's eyes across the barrel of the revolver. "I won't tell you again t' drop that sticker, mister."

The miner slowly looked from Longarm to the knife. He hesitated. Then very slowly his fingers uncurled from the handle of the vicious weapon and it fell to the ground, landing beside the dying man. His victim seemed not to see, not the knife nor anything else around him. He held the pink and gray coils of his own guts cradled as if he were holding a baby. The man's entire world was wrapped up right there and surely he must have known that he was already as good as dead. Longarm hated to do it, but he ignored the dying man and stepped closer to the one who had killed him.

"Turn around," he said. "Put your hands behind you."

It took a minute for the man to respond. Then he did. Carefully. He was trembling in obvious fear now that the incident, whatever it had been, was over.

With one angry swipe of the big knife he had become a murderer, a fact that was only beginning to penetrate.

Longarm slipped his revolver back into its leather and pulled out his handcuffs. The killer offered no resistance when Longarm snapped the cuffs onto his wrists.

"I didn't mean to do that," he muttered. "Kenneth is my friend. My best friend and partner. I . . . I just got mad at him. You know?"

Longarm pushed him up against the bar and quickly ran his hands over the fellow's pockets and down his pant-legs to make sure he was not carrying any weapons other than the Bowie.

By the time that was done, a group of other drinkers were kneeling beside the man who had been cut. One of them looked up at Longarm and asked, "Where should we take him, Marshal?"

Longarm already knew there was no doctor in Bennett. He paused for only a few seconds before saying, "Take him to that fellow's place." He pointed to the Mexican proprietor of the seedy saloon. "He let this get out of hand. Let him help with the consequences."

"No, no, he will die screaming in the pain. You know this, damn you."

"You tend to him and you take good care o' him, or so help me, I'll find charges t' bring against you. An' you know I can do it." The Mexican shut up. He did not look any sort of happy. But Longarm figured he would do what he was told, and if there was screaming—and there would be—he was the one who would be discomforted by it.

"Go ahead. Carry him there an' make him as comfortable as you can."

"Aren't you going to . . ." one of the men began.

"I got t' tend to this here prisoner," Longarm said, indicating the handcuffed miner, who was now sniffling and sobbing as the realization of what he had done sank in.

"You won't . . . you won't hang me. Or anything. Will you?"

"Me? Hell no. I ain't gonna hang you. But a proper court an' judge most likely will. Now come along with me. There's no jail handy and I got t' figure out what I'm gonna do with you."

Longarm took the man by the elbow and guided him out of the saloon into the crisp, cool air of the high country evening.

Chapter 11

Longarm shoved his docile prisoner along to Bud Walker's saloon, largely because he did not either like or trust the Mexican but did trust Walker. Ted was behind the bar when he got there. There was no sign of Walker.

"Find Bud for me, will you, please?"

Ted took a look at the handcuffed and downcast miner and nodded. He disappeared into the back and returned moments later with Walker in tow.

"What is it you need, Marshal?"

"I need a place t' park this jasper until the next stage to Hartsel comes through. A good chain an' a stout post would do since there's not a proper jail hereabouts."

Walker responded, "We might not have a jail, but we have a wagon park out back of this block. Other side, not down toward the creek. I'm sure I can scare up some chain for you. Take him on over there. I'll find the chain and join you quick as I can."

"Thanks, Bud. You! What's your name?"

"Ed Boyle. I . . . I never meant to hurt Kenneth. Honest. I never."

" 'Meant to' don't cut it, Boyle. Now move along before you piss me off an' I have t' what we call 'take measures' to make you mind."

"I won't be no trouble for you, Marshal. I won't. I never . . . I never meant to cut Kenny like that. You got to believe me."

"The ones you want t' convince, Boyle, will be the jury that sits in judgment of you. Now get your ass moving."

Boyle did.

Longarm found the wagon park easily enough. He placed Boyle on the ground, leaning against a fence post. Bud Walker joined them fifteen or twenty minutes later, carrying a trace chain.

"This is the best I could find," he apologized. "It isn't all that heavy."

"It'll do," Longarm told him. "When will the next northbound come through?"

"About noon tomorrow."

"Then I'll set out here with the prisoner tonight an' take him on that stage up to Hartsel, maybe on to Fairplay. I need to get him booked into a proper jail an' charge him with murder, which is a state offense, not Federal."

"Is there anything else I can do?" Walker asked.

"Matter o' fact there is. I'll need two meals brought over come morning. Can you arrange that?"

"I surely can. I'll see to it right off."

Longarm nodded and thanked the man. When Walker left, Longarm used the handcuffs to chain Boyle to the fence post then pulled a keg close to the prisoner and sat on it. He withdrew a cheroot from inside his coat and lighted it.

"I could use a smoke myself, Marshal. Or a chew if you have one," Boyle said.

Longarm ignored him.

From a distance they heard a scream. Then another, louder.

"That will be your good friend an' partner, Kenneth. Bad as it is for him now, it's gonna get worse before he finally dies. So you sit there an' you listen to what you an' your knife did to that man."

Ed Boyle began to cry. Very likely his pal Kenneth was doing some crying just then, too.

It was a long night, the silence punctuated frequently by the sound of Kenneth's screams. It was only toward dawn that they faded away and finally stopped.

"The man will be dead now, I reckon," Longarm observed, a comment that only renewed the flow of Boyle's tears.

Chapter 12

By the time dawn softened the night into a gold and scarlet sunrise, Longarm was gritty-eyed and out of sorts. Not trusting the trace chain, he had remained awake throughout while Boyle sniffled and then snored.

His mood was lightened considerably when Mariska showed up carrying a tray with two large bowls of biscuits and gravy—the biscuits fluffy and the gravy mouthwateringly good—and a pair of tin mugs of hot, black coffee.

Longarm wanted to wrap his arms around the girl and kiss her but he did not dare. Boyle was listening, and any number of eyes might well have been directed their way. All he could do was to take the tray and thank her politely.

"You're welcome." He could see in her eyes that she wanted the same thing but she acted polite and distant. "When you're done, just leave everything on the ground here. I'll come collect it when I get a chance."

"Right."

Mariska went back to her father's tent. Longarm unlocked Boyle from his makeshift containment.

"If you want t' make a run for it," Longarm suggested, "you go right ahead an' do it. That'd save the folks up in Fairplay the trouble of a trial."

Boyle gave him a nervous glance and did not even stand up to stretch his legs. He remained right where he had been all night, reaching for a bowl and spoon and sitting down to eat.

Longarm moved his keg a few yards farther before he ate. It was unlikely that Boyle would make a move for him, but he was not willing to bet his life on it.

Breakfast disappeared in no time and coffee on top of it.

"I'm still hungry," Boyle complained when both bowls were empty and back on the tray.

"Tough shit," Longarm growled. "Get up now."

Boyle cringed away from him. Longarm was well aware that the man was not cuffed at the moment. And was aware, too, that however meek Boyle seemed right now, he was, in fact, a killer. Longarm intended to give him no slack.

"Get up, I said."

Boyle came to his feet.

"Walk down t' the creek. You know the way."

"I . . . you're going to shoot me, aren't you?"

"I damn sure might if you don't do as I say, you piece o' shit. Now move your ass."

"What . . ."

"We're gonna take up some o' that cold water an'

splash it on our faces. Leastways I am. Gonna get rid o' some o' the cobwebs."

Boyle moved quickly enough then, intruding on someone's placer claim long enough to wash his face a little. Longarm did the same and felt much better for it.

"Now back to the mercantile," Longarm told him. "I wanta find out what time the stage oughta come through."

"About eleven," Boyle said. "We have plenty of time."

"I'll check that with someone that doesn't maybe have a reason t' miss that coach if you don't mind."

Boyle was quiet after that. As well he should be, Longarm thought. He was facing a hangman's rope at the end of this little journey. Not right away, of course. There would be the trial first. Then a wait before the sentence was carried out. The very best he could hope for if he had a really good defense would be twenty-five to life. Considering the conditions given a lifer in the state prison at Canon City, Longarm was not sure but what he would prefer the rope.

"Turn around. I need t' get those cuffs back on you now."

Boyle complied without causing any trouble and led the way back to the store, where the stagecoach would stop later in the morning.

Longarm climbed down out of the coach, glad to be back on solid ground that did not jolt and bounce with every turn of the wheels. He looked around—not that there was so very much to see in Hartsel, just the hotel, the mud baths, and a couple stores—then reached up to take hold

of Boyle's arm and guide him down, Boyle's hands still
being cuffed behind his back.

The prisoner looked like he was about to break into
tears again. Once they got under way in Bennett, he cried
halfway north to Hartsel.

"Come along," Longarm ordered and led the man
into the shack that served as a stagecoach stop here.

"Something I can do for you, mister?" the agent asked.

"Aye, there is," Longarm said with a nod. "The next
coach over to Fairplay. When would that be?"

"You've already missed it for this morning. There
will be another tonight about nine."

Longarm grunted. "That's too long. I'm wanting t'
get rid of this fella. Got to turn him over to the county
sheriff. How's about I rent that buggy I see setting outside."

"I'm sorry, mister. That's my own outfit and I don't
rent it out to strangers."

Longarm pulled out his wallet and flipped it open to
display his badge. "It's official business, friend."

The agent glanced at the badge and asked, "Are you
Long?"

"I am. Why?"

The man rummaged in a box on top of his desk and
brought out a folded sheet of yellow paper. "Telegram
came for you last night, that's why. I was going to send
it down to you in Bennett on the next coach south." He
handed the message form across.

"Thanks. Now about that buggy?"

"You say it is official business?"

Longarm nodded. "We have a murderer here. He needs
to be behind bars."

"In that case, sure, I'll hook my mare up to the poles and you can drive. You know the way, I suppose."

"I do. And I thank you. I'll give you a voucher so you can be paid for the use of your rig."

"Five minutes," the agent said. He left the shack and Longarm opened the message.

"It looks like I have a couple more days t' get ready for that visit," he mumbled aloud to Boyle. "Says here the Cranston gang was spotted in Raton, headed north o' course. That gives me time t' turn you over to the law in Fairplay an' get back in plenty o' time to meet the Cranstons." He grinned. "Maybe you're lucky t' be out of there. Says there's eight of them on their way."

Oddly, Edward Boyle did not much look like he felt fortunate.

"Come along," Longarm said, taking the man by the arm. "Let's get you to Fairplay an' a proper set o' bars to put you behind."

Chapter 13

Fairplay was as busy a town as Longarm remembered from past visits. He liked the place. It had a friendly feel to it and, situated on the edge of South Park, a naturally handsome setting with a ring of mountain peaks in every direction.

The Park County jail was on the top floor of a three-story brick building. Longarm had to practically carry Ed Boyle up the flights of steep stairs. When he got there, he displayed his badge again and introduced himself to the deputy on duty.

"The sheriff is down in Denver for a few days, but I can sign this jasper in for you if you want to hold him here," the beefy deputy offered.

"He isn't my prisoner exactly. He's yours." Longarm explained the charges.

"Oh, my. We haven't had a hanging since I came on the job," the deputy said. He gave Boyle a speculative look and said, "I wonder if the sher'f would let me open the trap on this fella."

"It would save the county the cost of bringing in a professional hangman," Longarm said, "and if you don't get it right first off, well, you can keep trying until you do."

Boyle looked like he was going to die on the spot and save everyone a great deal of trouble.

"Put him inside," Longarm suggested. "I'll start filling out a report for you."

That chore took the better part of an hour—he was not likely to be around come time for Boyle's trial, and he did not want to see the son of a bitch get off on some technical point—then Longarm went back down the stairs and walked over to the business district just south of the county building.

He found a mercantile where he had done business before and bought a supply of cheroots, then went next door to a friendly little café for an overdue supper, as he had not had a chance to eat anything since he'd had Mariska's biscuits and gravy that morning. He filled up on steak and potatoes, then went outside to smoke one of his cheroots before reclaiming the buggy and heading back to Hartsel.

Longarm had barely cleared the town limits of Fairplay, the twilight cool and pleasant, a cigar between his teeth and the prospect of another "walk" with Mariska in his mind, when he heard a shout and saw a man step into the road just in front of him.

"Stand and deliver," a man's voice called.

A second man appeared out of the shadows on his

left, just about even with the seat of the light buggy.

Longarm drew back on the driving lines and the little mare obediently stopped. The fellow at the side of the rig stepped in close and stood with a carbine held as if at high port.

"Hand it over," the man in front of the horse ordered.

"Hand what over?"

"Everything you have and be quick about it."

"I don't have anything you want," Longarm said.

"The hell you don't. What we want is everything you got. Now do it."

"You're making a mistake," Longarm told the pair of highwaymen. "A big mistake."

"That's for us to judge. Now do what you're told. We want everything."

"Well, shit," Longarm grumbled.

"Everything, damn you, or we'll shoot."

With a sigh Longarm did indeed give them everything. He flicked the glowing stub of his cheroot into the face of the one standing beside him, palmed his Colt, and put a bullet into the chest of the man in front. He shifted his aim and shot the second man.

The mare reared in fright and tried to bolt, but Longarm brought her down with a yank on the lines. He had to rise up off the seat to see the first man, who was down on his knees in the middle of the road. There was light enough to see that the would-be robber still had his pistol in hand so Longarm shot him again, swung to his left, and put a second bullet into the other robber as well.

"Dammit t' hell," Longarm grumbled aloud. "That's

what I get for ridin' around like I was some big shot instead o' taking a coach like ever'body else."

He calmed the mare and then with a sigh set about collecting the bodies of the two seedy idiots, one of whom groaned when Longarm tried to pick him up. It startled the lawman so badly that he dropped the fellow, banging his head on the graded roadway and wringing another groan out of him.

"This'd be easier if you was dead," Longarm told him.

The wounded robber groaned again.

"Listen, if that's all the conversation you're good for, I oughta leave you laying here where you fell. Where 're you hit?"

The robber seemed unable to speak, but he pointed low on his right side and on his left thigh.

"You're lucky my shootin' was off tonight," Longarm told him. "Give me your belt."

The wounded man did not move, so Longarm stripped his belt from him and used it, along with the robber's bandanna, to put a pressure pad over the hole in his side, that seeming to be the more serious wound. The lesser injury he plugged with a wad of tobacco taken from a pouch in the fellow's shirt pocket.

"That's gonna have to hold you 'til we get you to Fairplay. If I remember a'right, they got a doctor there."

"What about Jedediah?"

"Your friend is dead. By rights you should be, too. Count yourself damned lucky."

Longarm loaded the wounded man onto the seat of the buggy and the dead one into the luggage boot. He would have to drive them back to Fairplay and fill out a world of paperwork before he could head out again. In all probability it would be dawn before he got back to Hartsel and late at night before he reached Bennett.

He wondered if he was *ever* going to be able to crawl into a bed and get some sleep.

Chapter 14

Longarm awoke in the boardinghouse in Bennett. He had a headache from going too long without sleep and then sleeping too deeply when he finally had the chance. The town was just damned lucky the Cranston gang did not show up while Longarm was feeling like that. Apart from his head trying to pound itself open from the inside out, he felt groggy and somewhat detached from reality, like he was sleepwalking.

He stumbled over to the washstand, poured a little water from the crockery pitcher beside the blue-and-white basin, and dipped both hands into the water, splashing his face thoroughly. Water soaked the neck of his balbriggans and ran into the hair on his chest, but it helped to revive him. He fumbled for the thin towel hanging on the side of the washstand and used it to dry his face.

Bleary-eyed, he peered into the very slightly cracked mirror that hung over the stand. He looked like shit, he thought. And he needed a shave. Bad.

Scowling, Longarm turned away from the mirror and got dressed, selecting a clean shirt from his carpetbag and while he did so taking inventory of what was there. He was going to have to find a laundry soon, he saw. Either that or allow his smell to announce his presence before he ever entered a place. He lifted his arm and sniffed, wrinkling his nose and scowling all the more. While he was about the shave, he really needed a bath, too. He pulled his last clean underthings out of the bag and laid them out on his unmade bed along with the clean shirt.

The very first thing after breakfast, he decided, he would look up both the shave and the bath, then come back here to change into the clean clothes. Better yet, he would take the clean things with him when he went to find the barber and the bath. He did have a razor in his carpetbag, but the way he felt this morning, if he tried to shave himself, he would only cut his own throat.

He went down to a filling—if not tasty—breakfast of watery oat porridge and overcooked biscuits with sorghum syrup, then walked down to a shop that displayed a white-and-red-striped pole outside.

"Good morning, Marshal."

A man who was about to sit in the barber's chair moved aside saying, "You can have the chair now, Marshal. I can wait."

"Thanks, but you go ahead. I ain't in any special hurry. In fact, I could use a bath first if you got a tub for hire." He directed the last to the barber, a plump man whose ragged haircut suggested that he cut his own hair. Longarm hoped he did a better job than that on the paying customers.

"The tub is in the back. Let me get some lather on Harold's face, then I'll be in to bring you some hot water."

"It's in the stove here? I can carry it myself," Longarm offered.

"Sure thing, Marshal. Anything you like."

Longarm drew a bucket of hot water from the reservoir, steam swirling on the water's surface, and carried it into the back room, where a slipper tub sat on a slightly raised platform. There was already water in the tub, not too dirty, so he just poured the fresh hot water in with what was already there, stripped out of his clothes, and stepped inside.

The warm water soothed aches he hadn't even recognized that he had, and the fingers of soft naphtha soap cut away the grime and sweat of the last few days.

He washed his cock thoroughly—thinking of Mariska while he did so—and peeled back the foreskin to wash beneath it. He had no idea what a dick tasted like, but he was sure she would rather it be clean when she took it into her mouth.

And thinking about that made him get hard, the warm water encouraging that.

He was about half tempted to finish what thoughts of the girl had started. But he could wait. Tonight when her father closed the café, he hoped.

And wouldn't it have been nice to have Mariska in the tub with him. He visualized washing her tits, shiny wet from the bathwater. Nipples hard. Belly flat and pubic hair matted and moist.

Oh, shit, he thought.

He wondered if the girl could get away for a quick

romp this morning before the lunch crowd started in.

No, dammit, he sternly reminded himself. Have some patience.

But it never hurt to think about such, he decided.

He was whistling when he put his clean clothes on and emerged into the barbershop end of the building.

Chapter 15

Longarm sat hunched over his second breakfast, this one oat porridge again but better tasting than the boarding-house meal had been.

"You do not eat much," Mariska whispered as she leaned over him, pretending to pour coffee into an al-ready full cup, her left tit pressing against his shoulder.

"I'll explain later. Is there any chance you can get away for a few hours this morning?" He'd thought he had the raging beast under control until evening, but that was until he saw Mariska there in her father's tent. She was modestly dressed, but Longarm's imagination saw her naked and moist, the way she had been in the aspen grove the previous evening.

"It might be possi . . . oh, probably not."

"Tell your father I offered to hire you as a guide here-abouts."

"What is this word 'hereaboot'?"

"Hereabouts," he said. "Means 'around here.' D'you think he'd let me hire you?"

"You would pay?"

"Not much, but sure. Be worth it t' get you off by myself."

"Shh," she cautioned. "Not so loud."

"Sorry. So will you ask him?"

The girl nodded. "I will ask."

She took the coffeepot back to the stove, where another one just like it was over the hot, glowing stovebox. She spoke with her father in that language again—Turkish, she had said—and very quickly came back. Longarm knew her old man's answer from the speed with which she returned. And from her sorrowful expression.

"He said no, didn't he?"

"Yes. I mean . . . no. My papa says no, I have work to do here to be ready for the lunch."

"All right. Thank you then," he said in a normal speaking voice and, softer, added, "Tonight?"

Mariska glanced first toward her father, then nodded. "After we close."

"I'll be lookin' forward to that all day long." Longarm left what remained of his meal, laid his napkin down, and placed a coin beside his bowl. He winked at the girl and whispered, "Later."

She looked as pleased as if he had just given her a present.

Longarm stepped outside, stretched hugely, and yawned so wide his jaw hurt. Then he began hiking upstream along the little creek where gold had been found to start the Bennett run, such as it was. It really was not a very big run or a very important one.

He had no trouble finding Clete Thomas's diggings. For one thing he had walked past the place yesterday on his way to the whorehouse.

It occurred to him that he might stop there again when he was finished speaking with Thomas. The madam ought to be in early in the day. He still wanted to talk to her about Ben Cranston. If anyone in Bennett knew anything about the young man, it should be the town madam.

First, though, he needed to speak with Thomas to see if he knew anything more than the general run of information. Longarm reasoned that a man in Thomas's position might well hear things that most folks didn't. Certainly it was worth a few minutes of his time to find out.

Unlike the other claims ranging up and down the creek, Thomas's digging was actually that. A dig.

Clete Thomas had dammed the normal flow of water and built a retaining wall to divert the flow around a sort of open pit, where large quantities of gravel containing small amounts of gold were dug out of the earth that originally was creek bed.

The main flow of the creek ran across an oversized sluice, where gravel and gold were separated, the water continuing downstream in the original bed, where the placer miners used it in the same way but on a smaller scale than Thomas's operation.

The disadvantage was that if the retaining wall ever gave way, whoever was at the bottom of the dig would very likely drown. In the meantime a crew of a dozen or more were busy extracting gravel, lifting it to the surface in buckets, and dumping it onto the sloping riffles of the giant sluice box.

High on the creek bank was a shack, which Longarm assumed would be the mine office, while higher still was a two-story house with a wraparound porch. The house was surrounded by outbuildings and sheds of various sorts. Not exactly a mansion but mighty grand for a little camp like Bennett.

That, he was sure, would be the Thomas residence.

He headed off in search of Bennett's leading citizen.

Chapter 16

The front door was opened before he got up the steps to the porch, and two young girls came pouring out like a pair of puppies let out of a kennel. Longarm guessed their age at thirteen or fourteen, barely old enough to have tits or hair on their pussies but plenty old enough to be saucy.

"You're the new marshal, aren't you?"

"Are you going to put handcuffs on me? I think I'd like that."

"Do you think I'm pretty?"

"Hush your mouth. He came to see me, not you."

Longarm managed to wedge a breath into their stream of chatter. "I came to see your daddy. And I think you're both pretty."

Both preened, practically bathing themselves in the compliment.

In truth, they were not pretty. Yet. Their features had not settled into what in adulthood very likely would be a refined loveliness. But now they were coltish and unformed, their complexions mottled with spots and freckles, their eyebrows bushy, and their noses rather flat. They had blond hair chopped off short for convenience, a lack of style that no grown-up lady would have allowed, and their clothes—denims and flannel shirts—would have been suitable for boys but certainly not for young ladies.

"Do you want to make love to me?" one said. The innocent way she said it made Longarm suspect she did not know the extent of that question.

"I kissed a man once. Do you want to kiss me?" the other said.

"What I want," Longarm said, "is to have a word with your papa. And you two should be careful what you say. Some grown man might misunderstand an' educate you in ways that you won't like."

Their lips pursed into a pout—both of them—and one sighed.

"I'm Betsy," the one on his left said.

"I'm Abby."

"Pleased t' meet you, I'm sure. Now can I *please* see your daddy?"

"We're more fun," Abby said.

"I'm sure you are but I got business with your papa."

"He doesn't go down to the office for business until ten," Betsy said.

"This isn't office-type business," Longarm told them. "It's marshal stuff I want t' see him about."

"If we don't let you, will you take us in and . . . do things to us to make us talk?" That one was Betsy again. He thought. They had begun moving around and now he was not sure which one was which.

"I don't care if you two talk or not," he said, "since

it's your dad that I want to see. Now please . . ."

They pouted again but one of them said, "He's busy, but I'll go ask if he'll see you now."

"Thank you."

Both girls, alike as peas in a pod, disappeared indoors as quickly as they had come tumbling out. Longarm shook his head in utter amazement. These two must be quite a handful.

He stood off to one side of the doorway and removed his hat, holding it in front of his belt buckle while he waited. He must have been there the better part of ten minutes before the girls—did they ever do anything individually or were they always hitched in tandem, he wondered—came to the door and said, "He'll be out in just a minute."

A minute stretched to five before he heard a door slam from somewhere toward the back of the house. Gravel crunched underfoot on the town side of the house so Longarm naturally moved in that direction, thinking it was Thomas coming out to meet him.

Instead he saw a pale green gown and matching parasol marching toward the path that led along the creek. He could not see the woman's face. He did not have to. It was the redhead he had run into the first morning he was in Bennett.

He could not help but wonder what business she would have with Clete Thomas. Lucky SOB if that business was the same thing Longarm's imagination conjured up.

His idle speculations were halted by the sound of the front door and a deep voice saying, "Marshal Long. Please come inside. My daughters said you need to speak with me. Come in and be comfortable, please."

Chapter 17

Clete Thomas was completely unlike anything Longarm
had envisioned. He had expected a physically large man
to go with the size of his influence in Bennett. Instead
Thomas was perhaps five foot eight and possibly even
less than that.

He tried to make up for it by wearing shoes with ex-
tremely thick soles and by wearing his hair in an orator's
bushy mass as well as having thick Burnside whiskers.
His voice was deep and powerful, however, and he had
the self-confidence of a con artist. Hell, perhaps he was
a con artist or had been before he struck his vein in Bennett.

Thomas approached Longarm with his hand extended
and guided him inside to a comfortable seat in the parlor.

"Wine? Brandy? Whiskey?" Thomas offered.

"I guess it ain't too early for a whiskey. A small one
will do."

Instead of fetching the beverage himself, Thomas

showed off just a little. He reached for a small silver bell beside his chair and rang it. Half a moment later there was a maid in the doorway. "Yes, sir?"

"Whiskey for the marshal, Nelda. Coffee for me."

"Let me change my mind, Mr. Thomas. I'll have coffee, too, please."

"You're sure about that? My whiskey is the very best. And my name is Clete."

"I'm sure, Clete. I'd 'preciate a chance t' sip your whiskey another time. The coffee will do this mornin'."

"As you prefer." He turned his attention to the girl at the door. "Two coffees, Nelda."

"Yes, sir, Mr. Cletus." She left silently. She was barefoot, Longarm noticed, and thin.

The girl—she was of some indeterminate dark race, not much older than Thomas's daughters—dropped into a curtsy before she turned away.

"I don't mean to be rude, Marshal, but I have business over at the mine. I need to see to it, so can we get down to cases here? My girls tell me you needed to speak with me. What exactly would this be about?"

Before Longarm could answer, Nelda was back bearing a tray with two cups of chicory-laced black coffee. No cream or sugar was offered. Longarm saluted Thomas with his steaming cup and took a sip. He didn't much care for chicory, but the coffee was not bad despite it.

"You were about to say, Marshal?"

"So I was. I'm wantin' to know if you know anything about that boy that was killed."

"Cranston, you mean."

"That's right. His brothers will be here in a couple days, and them boys is mean as a nest o' rattlesnakes.

I'd like to keep them from hoorahing Bennett, and I reckon you feel the same. It wouldn't be much good for business for them t' burn the town down around your ears. Maybe kill a bunch o' folks. You especially ought t' be concerned, you havin' those young, pretty daughters."

"Oh, surely they would not . . ."

"Surely they would, Clete. They done it before, that an' worse. Those girls o' yours would have all the chance of a mouse against a hoot owl."

"That is . . . disquieting."

"Yeah, I'd reckon it would be." Longarm took another sip of the coffee. It tasted a little better to him this time.

"So, Clete. D'you know anything about that dead boy?"

"Just what we all know, Marshal. We was drunk and rowdy. He passed out in the alley and froze to death. It's as plain as that."

"Right." Longarm took a big swallow of the bitter coffee. Maybe . . . if it had tinned milk and a bunch of sugar in it . . .

"Is there some reason you would doubt what happened to the boy, Marshal?"

Longarm thought about that for a moment. Finally he said, "No, sir, not a single thing." Not a thing he could put his finger on, he might have added but did not. There was just something . . . perhaps the way everyone's story was exactly the same, almost word for word the same. No doubts, no deviation. Everyone told it just like he'd first heard it.

And of course, that could be because it was the simple truth. But there was something niggling in the back of his mind. Nothing definite. But . . . something.

"Is that all you need to see me about, Marshal?"

"It pretty much is, I s'pose. Did you know the boy? Meet him before he froze t' death, I mean."

Thomas shook his head. "No. Never."

"I reckon that's all I need to ask you this morning, sir, seein' that you never met him."

"Then if you will excuse me, I have business to attend to in the mine office."

"Of course." Longarm set his cup aside and rose, towering over the little entrepreneur. "Thank you for your time, Mr. Thomas."

The two shook hands and then Thomas excused himself. His place was taken by the servant girl, Nelda, who came into the parlor and said, "Mr. Thomas says you should stay and enjoy your coffee. I brought you another cup. Not so strong this time. And these doughnuts. They're fresh made this morning, Mr. Marshal, sir. Mr. Thomas says anything else you need, you should just ask. Anything at all, sir."

"That's awful nice o' you, Nelda, but I'd think there isn't . . . or come to think of it, maybe there is. He said *anything* I want?"

"Yes, sir, that is what he said."

Longarm smiled. "Sit down here, Nelda. Have a cup of coffee with me and some of these fine-looking doughnuts."

Chapter 18

The girl glanced nervously toward the doorway into the foyer. "I . . . I couldn't. Please, sir. I wouldn't feel . . ."

"It's all right. You don't have to," Longarm quickly said. He understood. Betsy and Abigail were somewhere nearby. They could well be listening in on whatever Nelda might have to say to him. Obviously the girl was fearful. "I don't have an office hereabouts, but would you be free t' walk with me to someplace where I could take down your official statement? Take it down all legal an' proper, that is."

"Oh, I don't know . . ."

"Mr. Thomas said you should do anything I ask, isn't that right?"

She gave him a bright smile and a little giggle. "Yes, sir, he did say that. Anything at all, he said."

"Making an official statement would certainly be included, I should think."

She giggled again. "Yes, sir."

Longarm drank down a good portion of his coffee and set the rest aside. "Come on then, Nelda. Walk with me."

"A minute, please?"

"Of course."

She darted out of the parlor. Longarm wandered into the foyer and stood near the vestibule to wait for the serving girl. She returned in short order, this time wearing shoes and without the frilly little maid's cap she had on earlier.

Longarm opened the door for her and offered his arm once they were outside. Those simple courtesies appeared to surprise her.

"Where can we go to talk, Nelda?" he asked once they were away from the house.

The girl glanced over her shoulder, seemed to study the house that was now behind her, then visibly relaxed. "I have . . . I know a place. Follow me."

She led the way to a faint path that led away from the back of the Thomas house, across a field of wildflowers, and into a stand of aspen. When they entered, they frightened a trio of cow elk from their rest, the big animals galloping awkwardly from their bedground while a yearling calf followed.

"That grass over there looks nice and soft," Nelda said, "and it is, but it has ticks in it. From the elk, you know. We'll go on over here to where the trees are too close together for the animals to feel comfortable. The grass is just as sweet and there's no ticks."

"It sounds like yours is a voice of experience," Longarm said.

"Yes, sir. I come here whenever I can. To get away, like."

"I understand."

"Do you, sir? Not many do. Nor care."

"Why, of course I care, Nelda. You seem a nice girl. Very pretty and bright."

"Pretty? Sir, I'm nothing but a house nigger."

He stopped, scowling. "Why would you call yourself such, young lady? I meant what I said. You *are* very pretty. And you do seem bright and pleasant."

"Abby and Betsy make it plain who I am," the girl said bitterly. "I am my mama's shame and my daddy's burden."

"I don't think I fully understand that, Nelda. Your mother and father weren't married? It happens. It isn't supposed to, but it is a simple fact of life. If two people love each other . . ."

"Wasn't no love involved, Mr. Marshal. My daddy owned my mama, see. She was his slave."

"That has been over and done with for a long time now. Why, young as you are . . ."

"I am twenty years old, Mr. Marshal. When I was borned, my mama hadn't yet been set free. My daddy couldn't hardly deny who I was, seeing as she was a virgin pure when he raped her. Then afterward, well, he kept me around. Sort of as a pet, I think. After Mama died, he put me to work in the house and here I am."

"Clete is your papa?"

She nodded. "Yes, sir."

"And the girls . . ."

"My sisters. They're mean little bitches, the both of them."

"You look younger than twenty, Nelda." He wanted
to change the subject here. A compliment, however faint,
generally did the trick. "And you're very pretty." The first
statement was entirely true, the second one almost so.

"Do you think so, sir?" Nelda pointed to a patch of
lush, sweet grass and dropped onto the ground to sit.
Longarm joined her. "You are a very handsome gentleman. Do you mind me saying that? I mean, you being a
white gentleman and all."

"Why, you can say anything you like, Nelda."

"Would you do something for me, sir?"

"Of course. If I can."

"Would you, I mean, would you put your arm around
me. Like as if you actually liked me."

"I'd be happy t' do that, young lady."

Nelda sighed. "Young lady," she repeated. "Nobody's
ever called me 'lady' before." She leaned against his chest
and Longarm put an arm around her skinny torso. She
put her cheek on his shoulder and closed her eyes. "This
feels awful nice," she murmured. "Nobody has held me
since my mama died. I like it."

The servant girl lifted her face to his, and without
consciously deciding to, he found himself kissing her,
not quite sure which of them had started the act. And a
very pleasant act it was. Nelda's breath was sweet. She
tasted of . . . he was not sure. Peach nectar perhaps. Whatever it was, he liked it.

His tongue slipped between her lips, and as natural as
breathing, he found her breast, small and firm and tipped
with rock-hard nipples.

He lay her back against the grass and kissed her some
more. He was only mildly surprised to find her fingers

searching the buttons of his fly, then expertly loosening them.

Longarm pulled back from her. "Look, I don't want t' take advantage here. I wouldn't want what happened to your mother happen to you, too, sweet girl."

"My mama was raped, Mr. Marshal. She was a virgin then. I'm not like her. I'm not no virgin either. I get used . . ." She turned her face away. "He comes to me 'most every night. I got no choice about that. With you, it's different. With you, it's my gift to you freely given. If you want me, that is."

Longarm grinned. "I thought I made that clear by now."

Nelda's giggle turned into a laugh as she pulled his cock free and wrapped her fingers around it. "Clear enough, sir."

"Now get your drawers off. An' quit calling me 'sir.' That don't seem right. Under the circumstances, I mean."

The girl laughed again and let go of him long enough to lift her skirts and shimmy out of her drawers.

Her flesh was soft, her pubic hair black and gleaming with moisture that seeped out of the purple-red lips of her very wet pussy.

Longarm dipped a finger into her and she clung to him tight, her pleasure evident. He found the spot he wanted and gently massaged it. After only a few moments she shuddered, stiffening as she was gripped by a powerful explosion of sensation.

"I never . . . I never . . ."

Longarm quieted her with a deep kiss, his fingers still moving in and on her. When he felt the time was right, he shoved his holster to the side so the Colt would not gouge her belly then shifted over on top of her, his cock finding its way quickly to the warm, ready opening and sliding in. A bit at a time. Then deep. Deep.

And the slow, sweet dance began.

Chapter 19

Longarm rummaged through his discarded clothing to come up with a cheroot and a sulfur-tipped match. He nipped the twist off the cheroot and lighted it, then lay back with his head in Nelda's lap. The last of her clothing had been discarded some time ago, so he had a most enjoyable view as he looked up through the cigar smoke to the perky mounds of her café au lait breasts and dark chocolate nipples.

"I said you're pretty," he told her. "You're also damned good."

"Because I care for you." She laughed. "Don't look so frightened. I don't mean that I am in love with you. I just meant that I think you are a nice man and I like you very much."

He rolled his head to the side and kissed the girl's soft, brown belly. "Thank you." Longarm sighed and took another pull on the cheroot. When he exhaled, he said, "Y'know I brought you out here for a reason. Your reason was better'n mine, I admit, but I'd still like t' ask you something."

"Anything, sir. Ask me anything you like."

He looked up at her and chuckled. "Sir? You're callin' me 'sir' after all the fun we been havin' here?"

Nelda shrugged. She gently smoothed his hair back and ran her fingertips over his face. "Habit," she said.

"Habit I understand. Anyway, what I was wantin' to know is if you know anything about Ben Cranston. Did you ever meet him or know anything about him?"

Nelda frowned in thought for a moment, then shook her head. "The only thing I heard is that he was the one who froze to death behind Mr. Walker's place. As far as I know, I never met him. But then Mr. Thomas doesn't exactly introduce me to guests. He has me serve them, that's all."

"Interestin'," Longarm said, "that you call him 'mister.' He is your father, you said."

"He is, but that is only because he raped my mama. He fucks me, too, you know. It isn't like he acts as my daddy. Closer to me being his slave. The whelp he got off a slave woman. The only difference is that nowadays it wouldn't be legal for him to sell me on the block."

"Why do you stay with him then?" Longarm asked. "You are free to leave if you want."

"Mr. Marshal, you are a fine gentleman but—forgive me for saying it—but you don't know what free really is. Where would I go if I left here? What would become of a high yella nigger girl out on her own? I can tell you what would happen. Either I'd be grabbed off by somebody for his own pleasures, maybe somebody worse than my daddy, who at least doesn't beat me. Or I'd go work in some cheap whorehouse and have to take on any drunk with two bits and a hard-on." She shook her head. "Neither of them appeals to me, sir. Better I stay here than that."

"You are an educated girl, Nelda. Surely you could find—"

"Sir, I know what I could find. You don't. You never been a nigger in white society. I have. Every day of my life. I know."

Longarm held his cigar aside and kissed her belly button. Nelda squirmed and laughed. "That tickles."

"Good," he said. "We was getting' too serious. Tell me something, though. Is there anything I can do for you? Anything t' make things better for you?"

The girl pondered his offer for a moment, then grinned and said, "There is one thing."

"If I can," he said, "I will."

"Then let me see if you can." She reached down to his cock and began fondling it, quickly bringing an erection back.

"There," she said happily. "I see that you can indeed do what I'm wanting of you. Now get off my lap so I can lie back and open my legs for you."

Hers was a request that he found very easy to fulfill.

Chapter 20

"If you don't mind," Nelda said an hour or so later, "if those daughters of his get the idea I've been out here bumping bellies with you, they won't ever let me hear the end of it. Won't let their daddy let go of it either. There's a purely evil streak in them. It isn't just high spirits. They're evil."

"I'm sorry it's so, but you're in a better place than me t' see any such. What is it you're wanting me t' do, sweet girl?"

"If you don't mind," she repeated before getting to her request, "if you don't mind, I'd best go on to the house alone. Let them think I've been out here wool-gathering or lollygagging. I'll go on and you might could wait just a little while before you venture out from among these trees."

"That sounds fine by me," Longarm said. He grinned. "Truth is, you have me just about worn down to a nub-bin anyway. You go ahead." He pulled his britches on, tucked his shirt in, and stepped into his boots. Nelda knelt before him and helped tug the close-fitting stove-pipe boots on. "Me," he said, "I'll stretch out on this grass for five or ten minutes of peace an' quiet. Mayhap those elk will come back and I can get a better look at that calf. Goodness, he was a pretty little thing." He laughed. "Not so little, though, if I recall correctly." He lay on his back and laced his fingers behind his head for a pillow.

Nelda finished dressing, brushed herself off, and knelt again. She leaned forward and kissed the slight bulge where his pecker lay, then shifted position and gave him a deep, warm kiss, her tongue flickering into his mouth and out again before she stood and said, "If I act like I don't know you should I see you again, Mr. Marshal, please don't take it serious. That's just the way it has to be. But I will always remember the fine, fine man you are. I'll always think of you as my dear friend. Good-bye now." She kissed him again and was gone.

Longarm was a man who was accustomed to odd hours and catnaps to keep his strength and vitality up. He told himself to awaken in ten minutes, then closed his eyes and was asleep almost immediately.

He came awake, instantly alert, but instead of sitting up, he lay perfectly still while he listened for any disturbance. He heard nothing but the flutter of a bird's wings and, close by, the ripping sound of grass being pulled and chewed.

Longarm smiled. The elk had indeed come back. He opened his eyes and craned his neck. Two cows and a calf, likely the same stocky little fellow, were grazing within ten or fifteen yards of where he lay.

Elk always amazed him. Taken carefully, one feature at a time, they were amazingly ugly creatures. They looked awkward and ungainly, and an undisturbed elk could by itself sound like a small herd of domestic cattle as they clumped loudly from place to place. Yet they could run and jump through the heaviest timber like so many lithe, lively mule deer or could slink away as silently as an owl gliding from one limb to another.

Longarm enjoyed elk. Including on the table.

Sighing, he sat up. The grazing elk did not spook but they did give him wary looks.

Longarm crept out of the glade without causing the big animals to leave their afternoon snack.

With the passage of time—and the most pleasant dalliance with Nelda—his belly was growling for some grub. He really should walk over to town and get a bite to eat at Mariska's father's tent. On the other hand, he was already this far away from downtown Bennett—such as it was—and still needed to speak with the madam at the whorehouse. If he was going to learn anything more about Benjamin Cranston, his money was on that cathouse as the best place to find it.

Longarm silently ordered his belly to shut the hell up and walked past Clete Thomas's big house and diggings, on toward the urban sprawl of the whorehouse with its tiny cluster of cabins.

Chapter 21

It was the plump one who answered the door. She was not wearing her wig today. The real girl had thinning hair—so much so that it suggested she might well be diseased—and looked fifteen years older and not half as pretty as when Longarm had seen her previously.

This time the other girls did not come racing each other to get to the parlor and perhaps snag an early customer. This time they knew he was not there for one of them.

"What can I do for you, Marshal?" the fat whore asked.

"I still need t' see your madam," he told her.

"Miss Jessie isn't here right now. Come back later."

"That's what you told me the last time."

"Yeah, and it was just as true then as it is now. You want to sit and wait?"

"How long do you think she will be?" he asked.

The girl shrugged. "Could be tonight sometime. We never know when to expect her."

"But she will be here in the evening?"

"Sure. She likes to see the gentleman callers in and collect their money and things like that. She's generally here at night."

"But not always?"

"No, not always. But you come back tonight. She will likely be here then."

"Fine. Thanks." It was not particularly fine but he would just have to live with it.

He left the whorehouse and hurried back to town, where he found a nearly empty café with, as before, Mariska taking care of the chest-high benches while her father was busy at the stove.

When Longarm arrived, they were cleaning more than cooking, most of the lunch crowd having already been and gone. Mariska smiled when she saw him.

"No, don't stand there," she told him, shooing him away from the bench. "Come over here. I'm about to have my meal. You can sit with me and my papa. His name is Pavel."

"He won't mind?"

"You are special guest. Government man. My papa understand this."

Longarm removed his Stetson and followed Mariska to the side of the tent where some folding stools were placed close to the stove. The lid was closed on the crate of tin plates and cups, and the crate was now serving as a makeshift table for the owner and his daughter.

Longarm nodded respectfully and sat, hoping that the burly cook did not suspect what Longarm had been doing with his daughter when they went out for a walk. "Sir." He felt like a kid who was asking a girl's father for the first time if he could take her to a dance.

Mariska broke into rapid Turkish, the only words of which he recognized were "Custis" and "Long." The father spoke briefly in the same tongue, then Mariska turned to Longarm and said, "My father is proud to feed the man who will save us from the Mongols. He says thank you for coming here. What would you like to eat? Something special, perhaps? We have an egg if you would like that."

"Please thank him for me, but I'll have whatever is in that pot over there." He pointed.

Mariska began to giggle. She spoke again to her father, who laughed hugely.

"What did I say that's so funny?" he asked.

"The pot you point to is our dishwater."

"All right then," Longarm said, laughing along with the other two. "I'll have whatever was for lunch. Wherever you might be hidin' it."

Lunch was a pleasure, not so much for the quality of the stew, which was fine, but for the quality of the company. He could not talk with Pavel Cook, but the man was an accommodating host and a pleasant dining companion. Mariska, of course, was a more than pleasant companion, at the table and elsewhere.

Chapter 22

Longarm drew the girl aside after he paid—Pavel Cook tried to refuse his money, but Longarm insisted—and was on his way outside. He put his hat on and in a low voice said, "I don't know if I can see you this evenin'. I have to go question somebody that may be a witness."

"Witness?" Mariska asked. "Do you not know that this man die in the alley behind the saloon? There is no witness. He would be alive if there was a witness."

"This is just . . . I dunno. A hunch. D'you know what a hunch is, Mariska?"

She shook her head.

"It's, oh, a guess, you might call it. You know a guess, don't you?"

"Yes, I know guess," she said.

"Right. Well, that's what this is. It might be important. If I get done early, I'll come by and we can maybe go for a, um, a walk."

Mariska giggled a little at the idea of the two of them going for another walk.

"I'll come if I can," he promised.

He wanted to give the pretty Turk a kiss, but her father might see it and that did not seem like a very good idea. Not if he intended to see her again.

"Later," he whispered.

Longarm ducked low to clear the tent flap and, eyes still down toward the ground, almost bumped into the slender redhead he saw just after he got off the stagecoach when he first arrived in Bennett.

"Excuse me, ma'am," he said, snatching the Stetson off again.

Red was carrying a parasol, the curved handle hooked over her wrist. She stood for a moment appraising him. After a very direct look into Longarm's eyes, she dropped her gaze. Her eyelashes fluttered just enough to make him think she might be interested in him.

"Are you all right, ma'am?" The redhead looked nervous. Perhaps even afraid. "Can I help?"

"I am fine," she said. Her voice was throaty. Warm satin, low pitched and smooth. She could talk to him any day. Longarm felt himself growing hard.

"Look, if there's anything I can do . . ."

"There is nothing," she said.

"Perhaps I can escort you t' wherever it is you're bound," he offered, looking in the direction she had been walking. There was not much up that way except Clete Thomas's mine. And Bennett's whorehouse.

The woman looked in that direction, too, and seemed all the more nervous.

"It's all right, ma'am. I seen you come out of the

Thomas house. I won't peach on you. I'd count it a privilege if you'd let me walk you back there."

"Yes, I . . . all right. Please." She extended her gloved hand and said, "I am Mrs. Foster."

Longarm lightly touched her fingertips, bowing slightly as he did so. Hell, his mama taught him manners once upon a time. "Custis Long," he said by way of introduction.

"Oh, I know who you are, Marshal. We all do."

He replaced the Stetson atop his head and offered an arm to the lady. She opened the parasol and held it over her right shoulder while with her left hand she accepted his arm.

He felt himself quite the swell as he escorted the lady, careful to adjust his strides to her much shorter steps.

When they neared the Thomas house, he disengaged himself from her and again bowed.

"Thank you, Marshal."

"My pleasure, ma'am." He meant that, too. She was a looker. Elegant and cultured. And she smelled damn good. Her scent was delicate. Understated. She was pretty. And she had those oversized knockers on such a slender frame.

His pecker began to stiffen again. He'd had it under control while they were strolling. Now he felt like he was losing the fight to keep it down. To make an uncomfortable situation even worse, Mrs. Foster appeared to notice the rising bulge in his britches. She saw and quickly turned her head away.

"If you would excuse me, ma'am," he said, wanting to get the hell away from there before he embarrassed himself even more than he already had.

"Good day, Marshal Long."

"G'day, ma'am," he said, tipping his hat and quickly turning away so his erection would not be seen.

Since he was already at that end of town, he decided to walk on upstream along the creek to the whorehouse. He really wanted to speak with the madam of the place or with one of the girls if he could get one to talk with him.

Surely someone in this town knew more about Ben Cranston that they were admitting. The man—boy— hadn't just dropped out of a cloud before he went into Bud Walker's saloon. *Someone* surely had to know something about him, and Longarm's money was still on that whorehouse.

"No, Marshal, she isn't here," a pretty brunette told him.

"Then perhaps you—"

"No, sir. Do you want to know anything, you talk to Miss Jessie." The girl sounded firm about that.

This Miss Jessie, Longarm thought, ran a very tight ship here. Likely the girls would be disciplined if they spoke out of turn. He had known madams to be downright cruel if their rules were not obeyed, and he did not want to be the cause of any such thing here.

But dammit, he did want to find out if anyone actually knew anything about Ben Cranston. Or about the circumstances that led to his death in that alley.

More and more Longarm had the feeling that he was not being told everything.

And Bennett, Colorado, was purely running out of time.

The Cranston gang was entirely capable of destroying the entire town. They had done as much before.

Deputy United States Marshal Custis Long had been sent here to protect the community, but he was only one man who was being asked to stand against an entire gang of murderers. He believed he could hold his own against any man. Or any three men. But eight or ten of them?

He needed to find an edge.

And he wanted—needed—to learn more about the dead boy. If he expected to have any hope against the Cranstons, he needed to find something that would give him that edge with them.

He pulled a cheroot from his pocket, lit it, and walked slowly back along the creek toward the town, fretting that tomorrow or the next day it might no longer exist. Nor would its inhabitants. They all might be just so much ash and cinder, and wasn't that a helluva thought.

Chapter 23

Longarm tossed the butt of his cheroot into the street with a sigh. He simply did not know what to do. Other than to wait for the Cranstons to ride in with torches and blazing guns. One man, alone ... it did not look good for the future prospects of Bennett.

Thinking of Bennett, he turned in at the door to Titus Bennett's shop.

"Good afternoon, Longarm," the old man said, looking up from his workbench. "How are you today?"

"Not so damn good, Titus."

"Do you want to tell me about it?"

Longarm went behind the counter and helped himself to a seat on the stool there. He leaned back, his elbow on the countertop, and pondered for a moment. The old cobbler waited patiently for his guest to speak.

"Dammit, Titus, I'm missin' something here," he said finally.

"What would that be?"

Longarm shook his head. "Damned if I know. It's a feelin' more than anything else, I s'pose. But something is out o' place. The madam out at the whorehouse, for instance, an' the girls. The girls won't talk to me without her say-so and I can't ever get ahold o' her to ask her anything."

Bennett's eyebrows went up. "Really? Miss Jessie is almost always there."

"Every time I stop there, they tell me she's off doin' something else."

"What is it that you want to ask her?" Bennett asked.

"I'm thinkin' the Cranston boy might've spent a little time there before he got liquored up and froze. He had to've been some damn place, Titus, but no one in this town will admit to seeing him except in the saloon.

"One thing I do know is that a young man who's been traveling, which I suppose he was doin', a young an' healthy man who's been on the road, when he hits town, he'll be wanting a couple things. A bed to sleep in, a hot meal in his belly, a drink o' whiskey, an' a woman. Not necessarily in that order, dependin' on how randy he is and how thirsty.

"Now it could be that Bud Walker's place was the first he walked into, but I'm doubting it. Everyone says he came in there in the evening time, which makes me suspect he would've made at least a stop or two beforehand. Like a place t' lay out his traps for the night, especially it being such a cold night as it must've been.

"Come t' think of it, Titus, whatever happened to his gear? He wasn't on the road with just a saddle and a shirt. He must've had clothes an' camp gear an' like that. What's happened to that stuff? Who has it now?"

Bennett laid aside the needle and thread he had been working with and turned to face Longarm. "That is a good question and one I haven't an answer for."

"Did you see his horse, Titus?"

"I did. I remember that very well. The poor thing had been standing tied all night with the saddle still on its back. Someone . . . Bill Ventor's boy led it off, I believe."

"Do you remember what-all it was wearing? Saddle-bags, a bedroll, like that?"

"To tell you the truth, I don't recall. I'm sorry."

"Who is this Bill Ventor and where can I find his boy?" Longarm asked.

"The boy . . . I don't remember his name . . . isn't Bill's son. He is a foundling who helps Bill at his diggings over in the creek."

"Can you direct me to Ventor's claim?"

"Of course. I can take you there. I'll need to get back soon, though. I have to finish these slippers for, uh, for a friend."

Longarm looked at the delicately feminine footwear Bennett was repairing. He could guess what sort of friend the old coot meant. He already knew Bennett frequented Miss Jessie's whorehouse, so that was no surprise.

"Oh, I wouldn't want t' make you late with that job," Longarm said with a grin.

"Don't you be a smart-ass, young fellow."

"No, sir. I wouldn't think of it."

Bennett left his bench and flipped his OPEN sign on the door so it read CLOSED, Be Back Soon. "I'm ready whenever you are," he said.

Chapter 24

Bennett led Longarm across a flimsy footbridge that traversed the gold-bearing creek and on downstream to a muddy, much-worked placer dig that used a crude rocker to separate gold dust from the gravel.

A man of about forty with ferocious mustaches was working hip deep in the creek bed, digging up gravel from the bottom, while a boy of perhaps sixteen or seventeen poured the buckets of unsorted gravel into the top of the rocker, then followed that with buckets of water to wash the gravel and—they hoped—gold across the riffles on the floor of the rocker. The idea was that the lighter gravel would be washed over the thin wooden slats while the heavier gold would be left behind, trapped on the rocker floor. It was a system that could be built by anyone with even a bare minimum of carpentry skills and operated by anyone with patience and a strong back.

"'Lo, Titus," the man said, standing upright and wiping sweat from his forehead.

"Bill, I'd like you to meet Marshal Long. Longarm, this is my friend Bill Ventor."

Ventor waded out of the creek to them and extended his hand. "My pleasure, Marshal. You should know, sir, that we are all mighty glad you're here. We aren't fighters, you see, and if that gang of ruffians comes to burn our town for something we haven't done, well, most of us will be like sheep scattering before wolves. Most of us don't even own guns. Clubs and shovels would be all we would have to defend ourselves with."

"I'm hopin' it won't come to anything like that, Bill."

Bennett put in, "The marshal here wants to speak with your boy, Bill. If you don't mind, that is."

The young man in question had stopped his work at the rocker and drifted close while the men were talking. As soon as he stepped near, Longarm could see why Titus referred to him as Ventor's boy. The youngster's moon face and vapid expression suggested he was mentally deficient.

Dammit, Longarm thought, Titus should have warned him. Likely coming here was a completely wasted effort. He smiled, though, and stuck his hand out.

The boy's handshake grip was surprisingly powerful. The young man might not have much between the ears, but there was nothing wrong with his muscles. If anything, he was unnaturally strong.

"You can call me Custis," Longarm said. "What's your name?"

The boy looked down at his bare feet and wiggled his toes for a moment before he spoke. When he did, his voice was thick and slow. "I'm Henry."

"I want t' ask you about young Ben Cranston's horse,

Henry. I'm told you were the one who helped out by taking it away the morning after Cranston died."

Henry paused to think, then said, "I did that?"

"That's what I'm told," Longarm said. "Do you remember the horse?"

"I remember."

"Was the horse saddled?"

Henry did not answer for several moments, long enough for Ventor to prompt him, "You remember, don't you, Henry? The horse you took over to Mr. Tanzy?"

"I remember."

"Did you keep anything from that horse, Henry? The saddlebags, a gun, anything?"

He shook his head so violently Longarm at first thought something was wrong, that he was becoming sick or having a fit.

"Henry wouldn't take anything that wasn't his, Marshal," Ventor said.

"That's right, Longarm," Bennett agreed. "I know the boy. He may be simple but he is completely honest."

"Do you recall anything about that morning, Henry?" Longarm asked.

Again the boy shook his head.

"I'm sorry to've bothered you folks," Longarm said. "I took you away from your work."

"I'm just sorry me and Henry couldn't help."

"I didn't know . . ." Longarm let his voice trail away. "Thanks," he said and shook hands all around again.

What he needed to do now, he realized, was go talk to Jim Tanzy again since the horse and presumably all its trappings had been delivered to him.

Titus Bennett and Longarm walked back over the

bridge. Longarm walked with him as far as the shop, where a petite brunette wearing a worn and slightly soiled gown was waiting on the sidewalk. Longarm recognized her as one of the girls from the whorehouse, one who had not seemed willing to talk with him when she was among all the others.

On a hunch he followed her and Titus inside, the cobbler opening the door and then standing aside for the little whore.

"I'll have your slippers ready in a few minutes, Honey," Bennett said. Turning to Longarm, he added, "This is my dear friend Honey Behr."

The girl laughed and said, "My name is pronounced 'bear' but it's spelled different." She spelled it for him.

"Say, Honey," Longarm told her, "since you have to wait a few minutes, maybe you and me could go over to the café an' have some coffee or something."

"Oh, I couldn't do a thing like that. I mean . . . you know."

"You wouldn't be comfortable out in public with me?"

She bobbed her head in agreement. The girl would have been pretty, Longarm thought, except for having very bad teeth and a rash of some sort on her neck and right cheek. A penalty of her trade, he supposed.

"Then perhaps we could talk here. Titus, you wouldn't mind, would you?"

"As a matter of fact, Honey," the old fellow said, "I would consider it a favor to me if you would talk with the marshal. You can trust him. He is here to help us. All of us. You and the girls included."

"If you say so, Mr. Bennett." Honey turned to Longarm and asked, "What do you want to know, Marshal?"

Chapter 25

Tanzy was busy with a customer, weighing out a quarter pound of copper nails, when Longarm entered the hardware. The nails would probably be used in the construction of a Long Tom or a smaller rocker, Longarm knew. Copper because they would not rust away from the frequent immersion in water the way iron nails would. He waited until the miner paid for his purchase and left before he approached the storekeeper.

"Mr. Mayor," he said, "I have a few questions for you."

"Anything I can do, Marshal," Tanzy said. "Anything at all."

"Yes, sir. Well, it's about the morning after the Cranston boy froze t' death. His horse was found standing out front, I understand, an' the animal was led over here to you. Is that right?"

"Yes, it is, Marshal. The town had some expenses because of the young man's death. The laying out, blasting open ground for the grave, things like that. I sold the horse and used that money to cover those expenses. If it matters, I sold the horse for ten dollars. Five of it went for labor to open the grave, a dollar for powder to break the ground, and the other four I put in the town treasury as . . . well, just on general principles. I hope that was all right."

"Fine as far as I know," Longarm said. "Or care. What I'm wondering, you told me before that you sold the horse an' its rigging. Is that right?"

Tanzy nodded.

"Horse, saddle, blanket?"

"That's right."

"What about saddlebags or bedroll?" Longarm asked.

The storekeeper thought for a moment, then shook his head. "No, I don't recall there being either of those things."

"Then he must've left them somewhere else in town before he hit Bud Walker's place, because he wouldn't have been traveling without some sort of trappings," Longarm mused aloud.

"I suppose so," Tanzy agreed.

"How many places in Bennett take in overnight guests?" Longarm asked.

"Well, there is George Jennings, of course, where you are staying. There is Levi Lewisson. He has the clapboard house the other side of Jennings's place. And there is Hardy Nichols. His place is the big tent next to Pavel Cook's café. Hardy offers cots, not rooms, but for a little extra you can have space enough to hang canvas walls around your cot."

"As a matter of curiosity, Jim, where do you live?"

Tanzy inclined his head toward the back of his store.

"I have my bed back there. I'd say most of us business-men live in the back rooms of our stores." He shrugged. "It's convenient and it cuts way down on break-ins. That is important since we have no bank in Bennett and pretty much have to keep our cash ready to hand."

"Cash that you may have to forfeit to the Cranstons," Longarm said.

"That's right. It's another reason why we are so glad you are here. We need protection from those people for a number of reasons."

"All right," Longarm said. "If I think of anything else, I'll be back."

"Any time, Marshal. You know I want to help any way I can."

"Yes," Longarm said, "everyone in Bennett tells me that, everywhere I go."

"We mean it, too," Tanzy said.

Longarm got halfway to the door before he turned back as if by afterthought and asked, "This dead boy. Had you seen him before he died?"

"I was in Bud's place that night," Tanzy said. "I saw him then but not to pay attention to. I left before he was thrown out."

"What time was that?"

"When he was thrown outside?"

"No, what time did you leave?"

Tanzy thought for a moment then said, "Around ten or so, I think. Is it important?"

"No, prob'ly not. You never saw him around town be-fore that night? He never came in your store here?"

"No, I'm sure I never saw him before then." Tanzy removed his spectacles and concentrated on polishing them with a handkerchief he pulled from a trousers pocket.

"All right. Thank you." Longarm smiled and nodded, then went on his way.

Why, he was silently wondering, was Jim Tanzy lying to him now? Because Ben Cranston had been in Bennett, Colorado, for at least a full week before he died.

Honey Behr had told him that much.

A full week. And no one else in a town as small as Bennett would admit to having seen him in that time?

That did not add up worth a shit.

One thing he was sure of. There *was* a reason.

He just did not know what that reason might be.

Yet.

Chapter 26

Longarm ate the bland and nearly tasteless supper at George Jennings's boardinghouse rather than give Mariska the idea that he and his cock might be available that evening. Afterward he went outside and settled into one of the rocking chairs for a smoke before he walked out to Miss Jessie's whorehouse for that much-needed talk with the madam.

During the afternoon he had spoken to damn near everyone else in the town of Bennett. Their stories were all nearly identical.

And nearly unbelievable.

No one saw Ben Cranston in town before the night he died. No one except Bud Walker and his bartender saw Cranston thrown out of the saloon. No one saw the body after it was discovered in the alley. And no one knew who sewed him into the shroud he was buried in.

Longarm puffed on his cheroot and thought about his conversations that day, starting with Honey Behr and continuing through most of the businessmen in the community.

He was fairly sure that Honey told him the simple truth. She had no reason to lie.

He was just as convinced that every other son of a bitch in Bennett was lying to him. And that meant they had some reason to do so.

Interesting. Mighty damned interesting, he thought.

He sat, slowly rocking back and forth and paying no attention at all to the other two boarders who sat in rocking chairs nearby, until his cigar was finished. Then he flicked it into the ruts that passed for a street and stood, his knees crackling.

"Going to bed so early?" one of the men asked, his voice displaying no interest whatsoever in whatever Longarm's answer might be.

Longarm grunted, a sound that could have been taken to mean anything the fellow wanted it to. Then he briefly lifted his hat to allow a little of the cool high country air to reach his scalp. Without speaking to the men outside Jennings's place, he stepped out into the street and started walking through town on his way to Miss Jessie's place.

Damn, but he did want—need—to speak with that woman.

He was thinking about Honey while he walked. If only the girl had known more. What she did know, what she told him, was just enough to raise his hackles, just enough to let him know that something about Ben Cranston and his death did not ring true.

He was about to pass by the Mexican's raucous and rowdy saloon when something—a thing so small he did not consciously recognize it—gave him the feeling that the skin on the back of his neck was drawing tight.

Longarm's gut clenched and his mouth became dry.

He stopped. Whirled. Dropping into a crouch, his double-action .45 in hand, eyes searching the shadows.

A lead-tipped spear of bright fire shot out from beside the flimsy building, and a bullet's flight sizzled past his left shoulder.

If he had not stopped when he did . . .

Longarm took time to thumb back the hammer of his Colt. A simple squeeze of the trigger would do that job for him, but the pistol was steadier, the trigger pull lighter, if the hammer was cocked manually. At a distance his aim held truer that way.

He saw a shadow shift slightly, and another flare of burning gunpowder came from the spot beside the saloon.

He had no idea where that bullet went. Not close enough to worry about.

The shooter had had two chances at him and missed. That seemed quite enough.

Longarm took careful aim and gently squeezed his trigger. The .45 bucked in his hand and another spear of fire rent the young night.

He heard a yelp of pain and the sound of running feet.

Instead of pursuing into the deeper shadow at the side of the saloon, he ran to the dim light inside the building, stepping in the front door at almost the same moment that a man wearing a cloth cap and dungarees staggered in the back way.

Longarm was fairly sure he had never seen this man before, but the fellow had a revolver in his hand and a bloody wound in his side.

"You!" Longarm shouted. "You're under arrest."

He badly wanted to take this one alive. He wanted to find out why a complete stranger was shooting at him.

The fellow gave Longarm no opportunity for talk. Instead he raised his pistol, the muzzle swinging toward Longarm.

Longarm had no choice. He snapped a shot from his hip, his bullet striking the fellow in the midsection and doubling him over. Longarm thumbed his hammer, took time for an aimed shot, and put a slug into the top of the shooter's head.

A red-and-gray pulp that had been the fellow's brains squirted out of his ears. He was dead well before he hit the floor, facedown and unmoving.

Longarm swept the drinkers in the place with a murderous look but no one moved to challenge him. They stood as if frozen, some with mugs of beer held halfway to their mouths.

Longarm took a deep breath and then another.

Very slowly he backed out of the Mex's saloon and into the night. Only when he was outside and out of the line of any more fire that might come from within did he shuck the empty brass from his Colt and reload.

With the revolver carrying six live rounds again, he palmed his wallet to display his badge and again entered the saloon, pistol in one hand and badge in the other.

Who the hell had the dead man been? And why did he want to shoot a United States deputy marshal?

None of this was making any sense, Longarm thought. None of it.

Chapter 27

"You," Longarm said to the Mexican behind the bar. "Who was this man?"

The Mex shrugged. "He drink here. He ain' my fren'."

"Do you know him?" Longarm asked the next man lined up at the bar. And then another and down the line until finally he came to someone who would admit to knowing the dead man.

"His name's Charlie," that fellow said.

"Last name?"

"I dunno. I wasn't his pal. Just kinda ran into him here most nights. I bought him a beer once 'cause he was broke."

"His name was Charlie Vickers," a man farther down the bar said. "He spent all he had to buy a played-out claim. Or so he said. Seems to me he spent more time drinking and bellyaching than he did digging."

"That's true," the first one said. "He bitched and grumbled a lot but he wasn't much for hard work. I guess he believed all that bullshit about finding gold laying around in the creeks just waiting to be picked up free for nothing."

"You and you," Longarm said, pointing to a pair who were idly watching with their elbows propped onto the bar surface. "Carry the asshole out back. You, go tell Jim Tanzy that the town has another burial to pay for."

"Me?" one of the men protested.

Longarm did not answer save for a long, hard look.

"I, uh, yes sir," the miner said, putting his mug down and heading for the corpse that was cooling on the saloon floor.

"Does anyone else have anything to say?" Longarm demanded. "No? Anyone want t' take a shot at me?" He waited a few seconds, then shoved his Colt back into the leather.

He did not, however, turn his back when he left the saloon.

Charles Vickers, he mused once he was outside in the cool of the night. The name meant nothing to him. He was fairly sure there were no posters out on the man, although just to be sure he would send Billy Vail a wire informing him of the shooting and asking for any available information on Vickers. Just as soon as he had a chance, he intended to do that.

In the meantime he was still wondering why a lazy piece of shit like Vickers would suddenly take a notion to kill a deputy marshal. Had the man wanted to murder Custis Long in particular or would just any lawman do to work off Vickers's anger with a world that was not giving him a free ride to prosperity?

Another question occurred to him, so he changed direction. Instead of continuing on toward Miss Jessie's whorehouse, he spun around and walked through the deep shadows beside the Mexican's saloon.

As he neared the back, he overheard one of the men who had been dragging the body say, "Shit, man, will you look at this?"

"Hey now, half of that should be mine," another voice answered.

"Right. We'll split it. Fair is fair, so you get half."

"How much is there?"

"I can't see in the dark here but it feels like, lemme see, these here coins feels like double eagles an' there's, uh, five of them."

"No shit? Fifty dollars for the each of us?"

"Move over a little so's I can catch the light better. Cripes, yes. The guy had a hunnerd dollars on him."

"So why did he want to rob that marshal guy if he already had a damn fortune in his pocket?"

Longarm leaned against the side of the building until he heard the two go back inside to celebrate their good fortune and drink much of it away. Then he quietly left without accosting the two. They had been assigned a task; they did it; it was just their good fortune to find so much money in Vickers's pockets. Longarm could not blame them for rifling those pockets.

What he cared about was a question he was sure neither of those two could answer: How did Charles Vickers come by that much sudden cash? Longarm felt reasonably sure he already knew the answer to that. He was assuming it was payment for the murder of Custis Long. But who paid it? And why?

Chapter 28

"No, sir, she isn't here," the fake redhead told him.

Longarm glanced over her shoulder, half expecting to see Miss Jessie lurking around a corner or behind a drape. He did not. If the house madam was in, she was not making an appearance for Longarm's sake.

He debated whether there was any point to asking when Miss Jessie would return, then decided against it. He more than half believed the madam had been here all along but chose not to speak with him.

If true, that was, of course, her right. She was not under arrest for anything or even under suspicion, and if she wanted to clam up, well, there was not a damn thing he could do about it.

But he did not have to like it.

"All right. Thanks."

The girl smiled—what is it about these whores that they had such rotten teeth; did semen have some sort of caustic effect on tooth enamel?—and asked, "Would you like a good fuck, Marshal? I'm awfully good. Everyone says so."

"Thanks, but I don't have time t'night. I'm on duty, y'see."

"Another time then," she said. "It's only a dollar."

Like hell a dollar, he thought. Fifty cents was more like it. Not that he would be interested at that amount either. Screwing her would be like sticking his dick into the sludge at the bottom of an outhouse.

He lightly touched the brim of his Stetson and pretended not to notice Jim Tanzy sitting on the parlor sofa with the fat blonde on his knee.

Longarm headed back to town. As he passed the Thomas diggings, he thought about Nelda, Thomas's mulatto daughter. He liked that girl and wished there was something he could do to improve her situation. She was right, though. If she went down to Denver or to high-toned Colorado Springs, the only work a girl in her situation could find would be whoring, and that would be even worse than where she was now. At least with Thomas she had to contend with the wants and needs of only one man. In the city she would have to take on a dozen a day or more and some of those drunk and abusive.

No, she was better off here, being laid by her own father whenever he wanted her.

That was a hard thing to say but it was true.

Longarm did not have to like it, though.

He also gave passing thought to Thomas's other daughters, Abigail and Betsy. Those two would not fare well if the Cranstons succeeded in hoorahing Bennett.

He had no reason to particularly care about them, but

he certainly had no ill will for them either. He hoped they would survive whatever happened here in Bennett, Colorado.

Longarm stuck the end of a cheroot between his teeth and grinned around it.

The fact of the matter was that he hoped *he* survived whatever was going to happen here, too.

One man against that many . . . his prospects would not be good.

He quickened his pace. Of a sudden he wanted to find Mariska Cook and see if she could get away from her father's café for a little while.

Chapter 29

Longarm stroked the back of Mariska's head, smoothing her hair and gently caressing the back of her neck.

He had his eyes closed while he concentrated on the feel of his dick being surrounded by the wet heat of the girl's mouth as she sucked him, alternately taking him deep into her mouth then withdrawing slightly to run her tongue around and around the head of his cock.

The girl did know how to please a man.

He sighed his satisfaction, then tugged her away from her chore, the night air chill on his prick where it was coated with her saliva. Longarm pulled her down onto her back and rolled on top of her.

Mariska opened her legs to him and he slid deep into her pussy. The girl murmured softly into his ear as he began to stroke, a wordless litany of sensations. Her hips rose to meet him and her belly slapped wetly against his.

The pace of their coupling was slow and languid at first, then it built, faster and faster, harder and deeper, until he was slamming her onto the ground beneath him, driving into a frenzy of pleasure, both of them grunting with effort as one strove to engulf the other.

At last Mariska cried out, unable to contain the sheer force of her climax. When he felt her flesh clench tight around his shaft, Longarm, too, reached orgasm, his fluids bursting out deep inside the girl's body. He held himself stiff above her while he pumped jism in wave after wave. When finally he was done, he collapsed on top of her, the girl's slight form easily accommodating his weight.

Longarm chuckled. "You have bony hips," he said, laughing. "D'you know that?"

"You have something else that is bony. Do *you* know *that*?"

"Yeah," he said, "and I'm damn glad of it."

She kissed the side of his neck and ran her tongue into his ear. "So am I," she whispered.

Longarm kissed the girl long and gently, then rolled off her onto the now crushed and rather matted grass in their little aspen glade. He lay on his back while Mariska idly toyed with his cock and his balls.

"Only one time this night?" she teased.

"Are we in a hurry?"

"There is no hurry, no."

"Tell me something," he said. "You know . . . I don't know what 'tis that you know, lass, but you do know somethin'. Something that a girlfriend has told you would be my guess, and I got a hunch that that something is a something that I oughta know before that gang of cutthroats an' killers comes ridin' through here shooting an' looting an' raising hell in general. I need t' know everything I can, girl. I'm askin' you to help me."

Mariska lay her head against Longarm's bare chest, her breath warm on his skin. She stayed like that for some time. She seemed to be in thought, and he left her alone to work out whatever it was that she was thinking.

Finally she rose up and looked at him closely. "I made a promise," she said.

"An' you meant it," he told her, "but I got t' know, honey. People's lives could depend on it."

Again she hesitated. Then Mariska said, "I do not know much. But I do know this dead man had a girlfriend here. Not my good friend but someone she knows, I don't know who. And . . . and once I heard a man in my papa's café say he helped to bury this dead man and . . . and he was not froze like they say but was shot. In the head. I hear this because this man, this man at the café, he was sick looking at the porridge. He says it reminds him of the . . . the brains of this dead man Billy Cranston."

Longarm sat bolt upright, the sudden movement shoving Mariska rudely aside. "Sorry," he said, steadying her. "Are you sure o' that?"

"I am sure it is what I heard, yes. But I did not see this for myself. You know?"

"Right, but . . . that would make one helluva big difference, honey. Listen, we'll have t' continue this another time. Right now there's something I got t' do."

With that, he stood and began pulling his clothes on.

Chapter 30

Longarm took Mariska by the wrist and began tugging her along behind him like a puppy on a leash.

"Where are we going?" she protested. "I don't want my father to see."

"It's all right. If he does see an' asks anything, I'll just tell him that it's official United States gummint business. Which is the natural truth."

"Official what?"

"You'll see," he assured her. "Come along now. We got t' see if Jim Tanzy has got home yet from his visit out to Miss Jessie's place."

"I know Mr. Tanzy. He eats with us. Nice man."

"Good 'cause I got t' ask some favors of him," Longarm said.

He led her down into Bennett and across the street to Tanzy's Hardware and Mining Supply Store. The door was locked and the place dark at that hour, but Longarm pounded on the door and called out for the owner. After several long minutes a bleary-eyed and not very happy proprietor showed up.

"What the hell do . . . oh, it's you, Longarm." Tanzy noticed Mariska Cook standing beside Longarm and quickly looked down at his nightshirt to make sure nothing was showing that shouldn't be. "What do you want, Longarm? Do you know it's the middle of the night?"

Longarm ignored the rhetorical questions and got down to the real one. "Jim, I need t' borrow a lantern. A full one, mind. An' a spade. Can you help me?"

"Of course I can. Do you mind if I ask why you need these things?"

"I suspect you already are guessin' the answer to that, Jim. I figure t' dig the boy up."

Tanzy looked like he had just been punched in the face. He sagged backward a half step and for a moment Longarm thought the storekeeper might actually lose his balance and fall down. He righted himself short of that happening and said, "You know?"

"Yeah," Longarm lied. He did know, but only a little.

"All of it?"

"Enough," Longarm said, and that was a complete, bald-faced lie. He only knew enough to know that he needed to find out a whole hell of a lot more. And soon, before the Cranstons arrived.

"We were hoping . . ." Tanzy's voice died away. Then he swallowed and raised his chin, squaring his shoulders. "We thought it was the best thing to do," he said. "We want . . . we wanted to preserve our town, you see. Without Clete and his payroll and all the business he and his people bring, well, the rest of us won't be able to keep going. Bennett will fade into dust like so many other boom camps have. Folks will move away and take their business with them. In a year or so there won't be but a handful of people here."

"It's that bad, d'you think?" Longarm asked.

"I'm sure of it. All of us are, all of us who are in on the secret."

"In on the lie," Longarm guessed. "About Ben Cranston freezing t' death in that alley."

Tanzy nodded. "Exactly." He looked at Mariska. "You understand, don't you? Your daddy's café wouldn't have enough customers to be worth bothering with. He'd have to pack his tent and all his trappings and move on to someplace else."

"Why?" the girl asked, her brow furrowed and a frown pulling down the corners of her mouth.

"Tell me about Clete," Longarm said, trying to bring them back to the point.

Tanzy shrugged. "A lovers' triangle," he said. "It was as simple as that. Or really not even a triangle, though Clete thought of it as one. The truth was that she was in love with the boy." Tanzy scowled. "I shouldn't keep on calling him a boy. He was young, but he was a man grown. Man enough to know who and what he wanted. He was going to marry her. She said he asked her . . . that was why she said she wanted out from under Clete, and I believe her about that . . . but you know Clete. Or I suppose you don't.

"That is part of the problem, you see. Clete thinks he owns people just like he owns things," Tanzy said. "He has never learned to let go. Not of things, not of the people in his life. When she wanted to leave Clete for the Cranston boy, he became furious. He grabbed a gun and threatened her. Said he would kill her before he saw her with another man.

"She ran away from him. Ran back to her own place. Cranston was staying there with her. I think the two of them might have known each other before. Maybe they were lovers. I'll never know nor need to. Anyway, she ran home. She told Cranston and he went to brace Clete about it. But not with a gun. He was just trying to talk Clete into letting go. Instead Clete got his gun again and shot him.

"I suppose it was easier for him to shoot Cranston than to shoot Jessie," Tanzy said.

"Jessie!" Longarm blurted. "You mean Cranston was in love with the madam of the whorehouse?"

"You didn't know? Yes, of course. That's where Cranston was staying. He was living there in one of those rooms. With Jessie." Tanzy paused. "You do know, don't you, that Clete Thomas owns the whorehouse. Jessie just works for him. As far as Clete is concerned, he may as well own her. He couldn't stand the idea of someone else having her."

"Well, I'll be a son of a bitch," Longarm said, then turned his head and said to Mariska, "Sorry for that language. I got a mite carried away." He shook his head. "Now I know I got t' meet this Jessie person."

It was Jim Tanzy's turn to look confused. "What do you mean? I saw you talking with her on the street the other day."

"Me? Hell no. I've never met the lady."

"Of course you have. Fine-looking woman. Redhead. The natural thing, though, not dyed."

"Red! *Miss Foster* is Jessie the whorehouse madam?"

"Yes, of course. Jessie Foster. Who did you think we were talking about?"

"Shee-it!" Longarm exclaimed. He shoved his hat back on his head and blew out his cheeks. "Shee-it," he repeated, and this time he did not bother apologizing to Mariska.

"I got t' go. Sorry to've woke you up, Jim, but it was awful important." He started to turn away, then stopped and turned back. "All the rest o' you, you an' Titus an' Bud Walker, all o' you, you cooked up this plan t' keep the Cranstons from knowing their kin was murdered an' they got their backs up just the same. Seems a helluva shame, don't it." He turned to Mariska. "Can you make it home without me escortin' you, girl?"

"Of course. My papa and me made it here all the way from Turkey. I can find my way across the street now, I think."

Longarm waited until Tanzy had closed the door of his store, then he bent and gave Mariska a quick kiss. "I'll see you at breakfast," he said.

"Be careful." She rose onto her tiptoes to give him another kiss, then whirled and ran lightly into the night.

Chapter 31

"Damn," Longarm mumbled. He turned and pounded on the hardware store door again.

Jim Tanzy was already awake, he probably had not had time to get back to his bedroom. This time he opened the door almost immediately. "What is it you want this time, Long?" He sounded annoyed.

"Sorry. I was so s'prised there that I forgot the reason I bothered you t' begin with."

Tanzy's eyebrows went up.

"The lantern," Longarm said. "An' the spade."

"Oh, yes. I forgot, too. Come inside then and pick out what you want."

Longarm selected a lantern and shook it, turned to Tanzy, and asked, "D'you keep coal oil here?"

"Of course I do. What do you think! This is a store, isn't it?" Tanzy took the lantern from him and carried it to the back of the room, where cans of coal oil were. He found a tin funnel and began filling the lantern while

Longarm found a spade he liked and took it to the rear where Tanzy was finishing filling the lantern.

Instead of handing the lantern to Longarm, though, Tanzy took it to his store counter, found a box of matches, and struck one. He lifted the bail and lighted the lantern, then handed the rest of the box of matches to Longarm. "You might need these. Do you need any help? Are you really going to dig up the body?"

Longarm nodded. "I am. But I don't need no help, thanks."

"Why would you do such a thing?" the storekeeper asked. "You know he has been in the ground for some months now. What you find won't be pleasant."

Longarm hefted the spade in one hand and carried the lantern low in the other. He said, "In a few more months, Jim, some judge over in Fairplay is gonna ask me how do I know Ben Cranston was shot. I got t' be able to testify, under oath, that I seen the bullet holes. It could be important, you see, an' I ain't one for letting murderers go free on account of technical shit."

"All right then. I suppose you know what you are doing."

"Now I do," Longarm said. "G'night, Jim. Thanks for the loan."

He headed out into the night, the bright flame of the lantern leading the way.

"Son of a *bitch*!" Longarm grumbled. It purely amazed him how hard this clay soil could get after just those few months of settling on top of Benjamin Cranston's mortal remains. Cool as it was, he was actually breaking into a sweat from trying to pry the ground loose over the boy.

Perhaps he should have borrowed a crow bar from Tanzy instead of a shovel.

He took a break, settling onto the lip of what hole he had dug so far. He reached over for the coat he had long since discarded, pawed through it until he found a cheroot, and let the coat fall back where it had been. He bit the twist off the small end of the cheroot, snapped a match aflame with his thumbnail, and lit the smoke. Lordy, but that did taste good. He drew the smoke deep into his lungs, coughed twice, and settled back with his hands laced over his knees and the cheroot between his teeth.

He heard the crunch of approaching footsteps and looked up to see another lantern come bobbing over the crest of the hill that lay between the cemetery and the town of Bennett.

When the lantern came near, he could see who was carrying it.

"Titus, what the hell are you doing awake at this hour?" Longarm asked.

"There is trouble," the old man said.

"The world is full o' trouble. What sort of it are we talkin' about this time?"

Bennett set his lantern down close to Longarm's and lowered himself to a seat beside the weary lawman. "Jim Tanzy decided to play both sides against the middle," Bennett said. "He called a meeting of . . . I guess you would call it our council. The group who know the truth about this boy who is buried here. He said you know the truth now, too. He thinks . . . Longarm, Jim thinks for the sake of the town we should . . . convince you to let this thing go. We'd like you to run the Cranstons off or however you want to handle them, but more important, we would like for you to leave Clete Thomas be. He owns too much here and contributes too much to what little economy we have for us to let him be taken in."

"I see," Longarm said, puffing slowly on his smoke. "You folks might've already guessed that I don't let go o' much. Little things sometimes but never murder. I won't allow a murderer to walk free, Titus. Not if I can help it." He grinned around the stub of his cheroot and added, "Somehow I just never got the hang o' backin' away from things neither. You can tell your friends that."

"Clete is talking about hiring you killed," Bennett warned.

"Are the others gonna go along with that?"

"None of us likes the idea. You should know that."

"But you are gonna go along with it," Longarm said.

"Once Clete gets an idea in his head, he is a hard man to stop."

"You could say the same for me," Longarm told him. He stood and added, "You did what you could, Titus. You came up here an' told me how this stick floats. I thank you for that."

Bennett cleared his throat and fidgeted a little before he said, "What I really came up here for, Longarm, is to ask you to leave. The reason you are here to begin with still stands, but we think you staying here and arresting Clete, we think that is a greater danger to the town than the Cranston gang is now."

"Yeah, well, that ain't gonna happen. There's a murder been done an' I figure to see that the murderer pays for what he done."

"If Clete can hire anyone to gun you, Longarm, there could be people trying to kill you."

Longarm snorted. "Wouldn't be for the first time then. An' I do thank you for the warning. I'll remember that when I'm givin' my testimony in court by an' by."

He reached for the spade.

"What are you doing?" Bennett asked.

"Same thing I come up here for, o' course. I got t' get this dead boy outa the ground so's I can take a look at him. An' then . . . I got me an idea what t' do with him when I got him on the green side o' the grass."

"Do you want to tell me about it?"

"Sure. Later. In the meantime I want you t' go back down to town. I want you t' gather up some pillows and a couple nice, new blankets. And a coffin. Got to have a proper coffin, not just the ratty old decaying blanket I can see down in this hole here. Let's see. You'll need them things. And a wagon, too."

"What are you up to?"

"You'll see. Go on now, please. I got t' finish getting this boy loose of the ground and go see does anybody want t' die trying to keep me from putting the cuffs on Clete Thomas."

"You would really—"

"Damn right I would. An' I will. You can tell them that if you like. See how anxious they are t' get a bullet in the belly on Thomas's behalf."

Bennett gave Longarm a nervous look, then picked up his lantern and hurried away.

Chapter 32

The lights in Bud Walker's saloon were still burning. It was not far short of dawn, yet there was something going on in there.

Longarm could pretty well guess what would be keeping people awake and jawing.

In a way he was glad. At least he could get a look at who was turning against him in Bennett now that he was in on the dirty little secret.

He headed straight for Walker's and in through the door.

Walker was there, of course, along with Jim Tanzy, George Jennings, and three men Longarm did not know. Those three were placer miners, to judge by their thigh-high rubber boots. There was no sign of Walker's bartender. Longarm would have expected him to be part of the group, since he most certainly would have to be in on the lie.

They had been in low conversation when Longarm

walked in on them, but that came to a sudden halt at his appearance. He crossed into the middle of the room but stopped short of the bar, where the locals were huddled.

"Don't let me interrupt," Longarm said cheerfully. He stood squared off to the six men, his thumbs hooked behind his belt buckle—which put his right hand only inches from the walnut grips of his .45.

"Would you, um, would you like a beer, Marshal?"

"Thanks, Bud, but no." He grinned. "I just came by t' get some information."

"Then how can we help you?" Walker asked.

"I got two questions. First is, how much is Clete Thomas offering for my scalp. An' the second . . ." The grin became positively jovial—but with much the same sort of purring pleasure that a mountain lion exhibits before devouring its prey. "The second question, gents, is who among you is takin' him up on the offer."

"We . . . honest to God, Marshal, we . . . none of us . . . we aren't going to try to collect."

One of the miners spoke up and said, "That's what brought me and my brothers here in the middle of the damn night, Marshal. We work for Clete. We draw our pay from him, and you should know that we got families to feed. But we ain't killers. We've all three of us fought Injuns when we was in the Army. Maybe we killed some or maybe we didn't. It can be hard to tell when there's a heap of shooting going on. But we aren't none of us gunmen and we don't want to be. We came over here to tell Bud and Jim about it and see what they think we should do."

"Just out of curiosity," Longarm said, "how much did he offer?"

"A hundred dollars, sir."

"Each?"

"No, sir. That would be for the three of us."

Longarm laughed. "The man is a cheap bastard, isn't he. Thirty-three dollars apiece to put yourselves on the Fed'ral gummint's Most Wanted list for the rest o' your lives. Seems hardly fair, don't it."

"Like I said, sir, we aren't killers. We didn't want any part of that deal."

"But there are others who took him up on it?"

The miner hesitated for a moment, then he nodded. "Yes, sir."

"How many?"

"Two boys that we know about. There could be more."

"Where are they?"

"They're holed up down at the mine office. Clete figures to fort up there."

"He's with them?"

"Oh, surely he would be. He didn't say, but then he wouldn't have to, would he. I mean . . . it's him that wants the killing done. You'd think he would want to see to it himself."

"That sort," Longarm said, "real often does not want to see to such his own self. That's why he hires other men, men better than him, to do what he doesn't have the stomach for."

Another one of the miners spoke then. "He already proved he can pull a trigger, didn't he."

"Because of Ben Cranston?" Longarm asked. "The way I heard it, Cranston went to talk to him. Wasn't carrying a gun at the time." He snorted. "It takes a real brave man to shoot someone who's unarmed. And with his back to him."

"*Back*," the first miner exclaimed. "That's the first we heard about the young fella being shot in the back."

"Ask your Walker and Tanzy if you don't believe me. They helped to bury Cranston."

All three of the miners turned to the local business-men. "Well, Bud? Jim? George? Is what he said true?"

Walker looked defeated. His shoulders slumped and he half turned away. "It's true."

"We didn't . . . we were just trying to save our town," Tanzy yelped.

Jennings's expression turned hard—from shame, Long-arm guessed—but he did not say a word.

"Jesus Christ!" one of the brothers snapped. The first who had spoken, presumably the oldest, turned to Long-arm and said, "We're sorry we got mixed up in this, Marshal. We don't want no part of murder. Don't want no part of Clete Thomas either. It's a low son of a bitch that will shoot a man in the back."

"Shot him in the back and, once he was down, put the muzzle in his ear and fired again," Longarm said. "Made a helluva mess of his head. I know because I just now dug him up."

"If there's anything we can do, sir . . ."

"Matter o' fact there is. I got the body outa the ground but I need some help with the rest o' what I got in mind."

"Name it, sir. Whatever it is, me and my brothers will help."

"What about you, Bud?" He looked Tanzy in the eye and added, "I already know where you stand, Jim, an'

you should know that I'll be taking you in on a charge of
aiding an' abetting. Bud? George?"

"I, uh, I'm out of this, Longarm. I want no part of it. I
did what I thought was best for the community. After all,
done was done, dead is dead. Nothing any of us did
could bring the boy back. But cold-blooded murder of a
Federal peace officer? No, sir. I'll not be involved in any
such of a thing."

Jennings turned his back on the room, placing both
elbows on the bar and peering into his mug. He still said
nothing to anyone.

"Jim here was trying to talk the rest of you into helping Thomas again, wasn't he?"

Walker hesitated, but the oldest of the mine workers
did not. "Yes, sir, he was. That's what we were talking
about when you got here."

"All right, thanks." Longarm turned his attention to
the storekeeper and said, "If you got any accounts you
want t' settle or to make arrangements for somebody to
watch your store for you, you'd best do it now. Soon as I
have Thomas in custody I'll be back for you. I'll deal
with the Cranstons, then Thomas an' you and me can
drive over to Fairplay an' start the paperwork to get you
boys tried and packed off to prison."

Longarm smiled and touched the brim of his Stetson.
With his left hand, just in case the damned near impos-
sible happened and Jim Tanzy made a try for him.

"G'night, gents."

He left as quietly as he had come.

Chapter 33

Tanzy's Hardware was locked up tight, although a candle had been left burning for the owner's return. At first, Longarm thought about carefully slipping the tongue of the lock with his pocket knife, but given the little consideration he owed Jim, he just kicked the damn door open.

The candle flame flickered at the sudden rush of air but remained lighted.

Longarm gave a little thought to the situation, then did some nocturnal shopping. If Tanzy wanted to take inventory and make a claim against the government, he was welcome to do so. After he got out of jail. Longarm figured he would get at least six months in county lockup, maybe longer. An actual prison term was unlikely, but then with the law, strange things did happen. Much would depend on the Park County prosecutor and the mood of the jurors in Fairplay.

The first thing he located and slapped onto the counter

was a box of dynamite, the wax-coated sticks packed in sawdust. He found a small crowbar and used it to pry the lid off.

His next "purchase" was an only slightly moldy knapsack, still with the stenciled initials U.S. on the cover. He put a dozen sticks of the dynamite into the knapsack, leaving the remainder of the box open on the counter.

Next he "bought" a length of fuse. He grunted when he lifted a heavy spool of 085 fuse onto the counter. In theory, it burned at a rate of 85 seconds per yard or just under 30 seconds per foot. That should be about right, he calculated. He cut several yards of the material off the spool, wound the fuse around his hand to make a loose ball—not too tight or some of the powder inside the fuse could separate and cause a dud—and stuffed that into his pocket.

He also partially unrolled a bolt of light canvas, the sort that could be used to sew a tent or some heavy britches. He cut a foot-wide swath of canvas off the end of the bolt, rolled that, and put it into the knapsack with the dynamite.

Finally he found a small carton of blasting caps and dropped them into a pocket—a different pocket—as well.

He was nearly to the door before he remembered one final need, and so went back and grabbed a hank of twine.

Longarm was whistling when he walked out into the thin light of the coming dawn.

He headed, in no hurry whatsoever, up-creek toward Clete Thomas's mine, where his would-be assassins were reportedly holed up in the mine office. Although why they would want to fort up instead of going on the hunt for him . . . He snorted. Amateurs. Expecting him to come to them so they could earn their blood money.

But then, come to think of it, he had.

Longarm used the early morning half-light to advantage, helping him slip undetected to a spot on the uphill side of the office shack, between the office and the residence. Both the uphill and the creek-facing sides of the shack were windowless. The front had the door and the back had a window, but there were the two blind sides. Convenient, Longarm thought.

He laid out the things he had brought from Tanzy's Hardware and took his time assembling them.

The twine was used to wrap around the dynamite, three sticks to a bound bundle. That accomplished, he used his pocket knife to gouge the ends of one stick in each bundle.

Next he cut the fuse cord into sections of perhaps a foot and a half in length. Those were *very* carefully crimped into a blasting cap apiece and the blasting caps were even more carefully pressed into the end of a dynamite stick.

When he was done, he had four handy bombs, each with three sticks of dynamite and a fuse that should burn for just over thirty seconds.

He found a discarded nail cask and upended it. Longarm settled himself more or less comfortably atop the cask. The raised rim of the cask cut into his butt a little but it was not anything he couldn't endure.

He placed his bombs on the ground beside his perch

and extracted the piece of canvas from the knapsack, which he discarded on the ground at his feet.

Preparations complete, he reached into his pocket, pulled out a cheroot, and lit it with a match.

Then, to get the attention of the boys inside the shack, he drew his Colt and fired a couple random shots into the blank wall that lay some twenty or so yards below his position.

He reloaded the Colt while he shouted, "You aren't gonna do much good cooped up inside there where you can't see t' shoot at me, boys. Y' might as well surrender yourselves an' get this over with 'ere I blast you out inta the open."

"Is that you, Long?" a voice answered after some seconds of delay.

"It's me, all right. Now come out or else."

"Or else what, damn you?"

By way of an answer, Longarm folded the canvas into a sort of sling and put one of his bombs into it. Standing up, he used the glowing tip of his cheroot to light the fuse, took a few swings around his head with the makeshift sling, and let the bomb fly in the direction of the mine shack.

The bomb, smoke streaming off the lighted fuse, sailed accurately enough, hit the shack wall, and bounded off.

Longarm resumed his seat and watched the fuse sizzle and sputter. After twenty seconds or so the dynamite exploded with a thunderclap. Dirt flew in a wide spray but there was no structural damage to the building as the bomb had been too far away from the wall.

It likely scared the shit out of anyone inside the building, though.

"I asked polite, boys," he shouted. "Come out now, else I'll blow the fucking place apart an' you boys with it."

"You . . . you're bluffing."

By way of an answer, Longarm lit another bomb and delivered it. This one landed closer. The blast was just as loud, and some of the wood planks on the side wall caved in.

"I ain't bluffing, boys. Come out. Do it now."

His cheroot was becoming short, so he used the stub of that one to light another and tossed the butt away—*not* close to the dynamite bombs.

"You're running out o' time," he shouted.

His answer was a gunshot, the bullet sizzling past his left ear and the sound coming from behind him. From the direction of Thomas's mansion.

Chapter 34

"Shit!" Longarm threw himself down and quickly rolled behind the nail cask—damn, he wished the thing was full of nails now to make sure it would stop any bullets flying his way—and yanked his Colt out again.

He peered around the side of the cask but could not see who was up there nor, for that matter, exactly where the shot had come from.

A puff of smoke appeared at an upstairs window. Which answered the question of where, although not who. Clete Thomas, he figured. It pretty much had to be the bossman trying for a change to do his dirty work himself.

He heard the mining shack door slam behind him, rolled onto his back, and snapped a shot at someone's arm and leg, all he could see of whoever it was down there. He got a yelp of pain in response. Likely grazed the son of a bitch, he suspected.

Longarm rolled onto his belly again in time to see a glimpse of white at the upstairs window and fired at it.

Onto his back again while he reloaded once more.

Trying to hold off attacks from two directions as once was a pisser, he thought. Better to end this shit quickly if he could.

He reached out, grabbed one of his two remaining bombs, and more hopeful than optimistic, lit the fuse.

Longarm jackknifed into a sitting position, surging off his back without warning to throw the bomb about as hard as he was able.

The weapon sailed, sputtering and smoking in an arc, and landed on the roof of the shack.

It started to roll, Longarm watching in rapt fascination as it approached the edge of the roof and over, falling onto the front stoop with a thump.

He heard some shouting from inside the little building and then the bomb went off.

Before the men in the shack had stopped screaming, Longarm was back onto his belly with his Colt extended toward Thomas's mansion.

He could see nothing there, not in the upstairs window nor any other window or door in the place. With no target to aim at, Longarm took a chance that Thomas—it almost had to be the boss who was up there shooting down at him—was moving to a new firing position.

Longarm grabbed his last remaining bomb, jumped to his feet, and sprinted uphill, directly toward the mansion.

He reached the steps and took them in a single bound. Once on the porch, he charged the front door. It was not locked so he let himself in, barely stopping himself from the ingrained habit of quietly closing the door behind him when he entered.

The vestibule and foyer of the house were empty, as was the parlor.

Longarm took the stairs to the second floor. There he found a short hallway with two doors leading to rooms at the rear of the house and one on the other side opening onto a front room. That was where the gunshots had come from, but he was already fairly sure that room was empty now.

He tried the first of the two rear bedrooms. One of the twins was there, sitting up in bed wearing night-clothes and clutching the covers high under her chin. The girl screamed when Longarm came in. He backed out without bothering to apologize. A man entering her bedchamber was the least of the girl's worries, as that man sincerely hoped to put her father behind bars for a great many years.

The other bedroom resulted in much the same sort of exchange, except this time the twin was ready for him and threw a shoe in his direction. He supposed he could have retaliated in kind. Could have thrown a boot at her. He did not. Did not apologize to that one either. Did shut the door behind him and head downstairs.

He looked into the parlor again—one of the more sensible escape techniques was to wait until a hiding spot had already been investigated and immediately slip back there to lie doggo in comfort while the pursuers moved on to fresh territory—and then went back into the kitchen.

He found no one there or in the pantry and so he went out onto the back porch.

A still spreading pool of water from an overturned wash basin suggested Thomas had just come that way.

That was confirmed by a very pale and frightened Nelda Thomas, who gave him a wide-eyed stare and pointed around the right side of the house.

Thomas, Longarm guessed, would expect him to follow. Instead he raced back the way he had just come, through the house and out the front door.

Longarm slowed down there and tiptoed across the porch to the side of the house.

When he looked around the corner, he grinned to himself. Clete Thomas was there, all right. Crouched low and with a revolver in his hand, staring toward the back of the house, where he expected Longarm to come around the corner.

Wrong corner, old fellow, Longarm chuckled to himself.

"It's over, Clete. Drop the gun an' maybe you'll live. Keep hold of it an' you'll die here an' now."

Thomas froze for a moment, then slowly he looked around. What he saw was the muzzle of Longarm's Colt.

He placed his revolver carefully on the ground before him and stood upright.

Longarm pulled out his handcuffs and stepped off the side of the porch, dropping to ground level.

That, and the fact that the scattergun was aimed at his head, was what saved him.

Chapter 35

Longarm did not take time for conscious thought. He whirled to face this new danger, Colt leveled and his finger already squeezing the trigger.

He saw the shotgun and immediately fired at the person holding it.

The slim figure crumpled to the floor of the porch, the shotgun clattering onto the boards.

"Jesus!" Longarm blurted out. He had just dropped one of the twins. A fourteen-, fifteen-year-old girl, for Pete's sake.

She had shot at him, dammit. Tried to kill him.

Even so!

And the other twin was likely somewhere nearby. Would she try to kill him also? Lord, he did hate the idea of having to shoot a girl. Practically still a child. Not that the shotgun knew the age or sex of the person firing it, but . . . shit.

"Thomas," Longarm called. "Get over here. One o'

your daughters has been shot. You got t' take care of her. You got to take care o' the other one."

"My . . . Abigail? Betsy?"

Clete Thomas seemed to lose all interest in Custis Long or anything the deputy represented. In an instant he became not a desperate criminal but a terrified father. He raced to Longarm's side and scrambled up onto the porch, rushing to his fallen daughter.

The other girl crept out of the house to join her father at her sister's side. A pool of blood beneath the limp, ragdoll-like body attested to Longarm's accuracy with that bullet.

Thomas looked up at Longarm standing over the three of them. The man's face was pale and drawn. "She's dead," he whispered, tears gathering in his eyes. "My Betsy is dead."

Longarm kicked the shotgun away lest Thomas be tempted to avenge his daughter's death. The scattergun was a double and likely still had a shell in the unfired barrel.

Down by what was left of the headquarters shack a man crawled out of the wreckage. He offered no fight and Longarm carried none to him. It was Clete Thomas who'd tried to hire a murderer, and Longarm's beef was with him, not the stupid SOB down there at the shack.

The fellow sidled away a few paces, then turned and ran like the hounds of Hell were on his heels.

Longarm glanced down at Thomas. "Stand up."

"What?"

"You heard me, you son of a bitch. Stand up. I'm putting you under arrest for the murder of Benjamin Cranston an' the attempted murder of a deputy United States marshal."

"But Betsy. What about my baby here?"

"You're the one who involved your family in this, Thomas. Now stand up an' turn around. I'm gonna put manacles on you. Unless you resist arrest. Do that an' I'll beat you down, mister."

"You can't talk to my daddy like that you old . . . you old . . ." The kid—Abigail that one would be—could not think of a term vile enough to describe the man who had shot and killed her sister. She stood there sputtering incoherently.

"Stand up," Longarm said. "I won't tell you ag'in."

Reluctantly, Thomas stood, turned around facing the other way, and put his hands behind his back.

Longarm locked the handcuffs onto Thomas's wrists and contemplated putting his spare pair on Abigail. Not that the kid had committed a crime. Yet.

"Girl," Longarm said to her, "your daddy is gonna be up to Fairplay for the trial, so it's up to you now t' take care o' things here. Get Mr. Bennett to help you take care o' your sister's body. Ask Nelda for help with the layin' out and whatever else you need. Are you listenin' to me? Are you hearin' me, girl? It's time now for you t' grow up."

"I hear you, you old bastard."

Longarm nodded. The kid was getting herself together now, he hoped. Not that he could worry himself about Thomas's family. Not now with the Cranston outfit likely only hours away. But dammit, he felt sorry for Abby.

"Come along, Thomas. I got to find a place t' stash you until I'm ready t' haul your sorry ass over to Fairplay. Then we'll see do you hang by the neck 'til you're dead or do you spend the rest o' your miserable life inside o' prison walls."

Chapter 36

The town was just coming to life when Longarm marched its leading citizen down the middle of the main street in handcuffs. To say that the sight created a sensation would be an understatement. He hadn't known there were that many people in Bennett until they all came out clamoring to know what was going on.

He saw that Jim Tanzy was with them, so he shocked everyone all the more by clamping manacles on him, too.

"All right, folks," Longarm announced, "I know you have questions. I'll give you answers, but let's be quick about it. Don't forget, the Cranston gang is due here, likely this afternoon. First off, about Clete Thomas . . ." He proceeded to briefly explain why Thomas and now Tanzy, too, were wearing jewelry behind their backs.

"No questions now," he said when he was done. "We got no time for such, but I do have me a question. Is any of you willin' to stand up with me against John Cranston an' the rest?"

Longarm stood there. Waiting. There was no response. There were some embarrassed expressions. Some men turned their heads away or dropped their eyes. But there were no volunteers in response to that plea.

He waited a few moments, then grunted. Loudly and deliberately. "All right then. So now I know."

"Wait," Titus Bennett said. "I'll help."

"So will I," a voice called from the back of the crowd. A female voice.

The crowd parted a little, the men shamed, and Longarm could see Jessica Foster standing there.

If anyone in Bennett, Colorado, had reason to hate Cletus Thomas, it would be the woman who ran his whorehouse. And who was the distraught lover of the young man Thomas killed to start this whole thing. Yet it was she who now was offering her help to keep Thomas alive long enough to get him to trial.

"I'll help," the town madam called, "and so will my girls. Just tell us what we can do."

There was considerable foot shuffling among the miners and businessmen then. Considerable reconsideration of their reluctance to act when the town's whores were willing to do whatever they could to stop the Cranston gang.

"I, uh, I reckon I could, well, maybe do somethin', too," a man said.

"Yeah. Me, too." Longarm recognized that one as one of the regulars in Bud Walker's saloon.

Several more voices spoke up. Some he recalled seeing before either in Pavel Cook's café, on the street, in the Mexican's place, or elsewhere. Even the Mexican saloon owner offered his services before the rest of the crowd dispersed.

"All right," Longarm said to those who remained. "Let's see what we'uns can do t' get this town ready t' greet those brothers an' their gang."

Chapter 37

"But we don't have guns," a man wearing a filthy derby hat and flamboyant mustaches said.

Longarm grinned. "Yeah, ain't that a pisser?" He looked around, shrugged, and said, "Follow me, boys." With a tip of his hat, he added, "An' ladies."

The whores giggled. But then he gathered they were not accustomed to being called ladies.

The women proceeded at the front of the line as Longarm led the way to Tanzy's Hardware and Mining Supply Store.

"In here now," he said. "Are we all here? What d' we have . . ." He counted aloud, dabbing a finger in the direction of each person he saw crowded into the store. "Eleven," he said with a grunt of satisfaction. There were five whores—one of Jessie Foster's girls had slipped away between the street gathering and the hardware—and six grubby miners.

"All right, boys . . . and girls. Here's what we know. John Cranston and his bunch have been known to ride roughshod through towns down to New Mexico. Burned some places out. Killed folks. Like that. So we ain't dealing with a bunch o' gentlemen. These boys is rough. We got t' be"—he grinned again—"rougher. Or anyway they got t' think that we are. Now help me out here. I want you ladies t' collect all the brooms Tanzy has on hand."

He peered at the rack of them against the left side wall. "How many is that? Four? Then four it will be. An' I want those mops I see in the corner there. There's three of 'em? I want those, too. An' a saw. It don't have t' be no finish saw. Rough will do. There. That Swedish bow saw will be fine.

"An' somebody grab them two crates behind the counter and that ball o' twine." Longarm himself picked up an awl and two small wooden boxes from beneath the counter where he had seen them earlier. He looked around, trying to think of what he might have forgotten.

"You there, yes you, see if you can find some, oh, boot black ought t' do, I think."

"Boot black?" the man blurted out, his eyebrows lifting and skepticism plain on his face.

"Trust me," Longarm said, afraid he might lose even this scant handful of volunteers. "I know what I'm doin'."

That, of course, was a bald-faced lie, but it did not seem the right moment to admit it.

What he had in mind was a plan that called for equal parts of wild-eyed optimism, brass-bold nerve, and if the truth be known, plain and simple prayer.

"Now gather 'round, folks. That's right. Bring those

brooms and mops over here to me. An' the saw. An' that other shit, too. We got us work t' do and no way of knowing how much time we got before them boys ride in thinking t' do you hurt."

Chapter 38

Longarm dragged out his Ingersol and checked it for perhaps the twentieth time in the past few hours. It was 11:13 a.m., exactly seven minutes since the last time he'd looked.

He stroked his mustache and frowned. This would be a helluva lot easier if he knew when to expect visitors. The problem was that it took an experienced hunter to lie in wait for any length of time and this had already gone on for much too long. Any more and he was afraid he would begin to lose his "army" to a combination of hunger and boredom and fear.

Longarm turned his head and said, "Jessie, you know where everybody is, don't you?"

The tastefully dressed redhead nodded. "I think so, yes."

"I want you t' go over to Cook's café. Get buckets of lunch an' carry them up to the roofs."

"Custis! Really. I will tear my dress if I do that."

"There's other things you could tear that'd be worse," he told her.

Most of the Bennett townspeople who'd agreed to help him thwart the Cranstons were placed on store roofs. For some reason it had been the whores who were most eager to occupy those posts. The girls stripped to their unmentionables lest they become entangled in the long dresses they were wearing. Once they were free of that encumbrance, they scrambled up onto the roofs like so many children let out of school early.

Of course, that allowed them to display their wares for whichever of the menfolk might be looking, but Longarm did not think that was the only reason they wanted to help. They seemed genuinely excited to be able to do something constructive for their community.

"Go on now, child," old Titus Bennett urged. "Do what Longarm tells you."

The three of them were gathered inside Bennett's shop, Longarm watching by the window while Jessie and Titus stayed low behind the counter in case shooting should break out unexpectedly.

"Buckets of slop," Jessie mumbled as she exited the store. "To think that I've come down to this."

Longarm chuckled. Then his expression became serious. He turned to the old cobbler and said, "I want you t' take over if I should go down, Titus."

"You expect to be killed, Longarm?"

"Shit, no. 'Course not." And in truth he refused to consider the possibility that he might die in this next encounter. But he could damn well come out of it badly wounded. That was not beyond the realm of possibility.

"No, what I'm thinkin'," he said, "is that if I go down for some reason, I want you t' take over. Organize a bucket brigade to put out fires. Stuff like that."

"I would certainly do that without being told," Bennett said.

"Thought so but I wanted t' make it clear with you.

"If it comes t' shooting, I'll go first for John an' Albert Cranston. I hear tell they're the he-coons of the outfit. Then Louis. An' after them three, well, whoever is left on his feet."

"Do you know these people?" Bennett asked.

Longarm shook his head but kept his eyes on the road leading into the town. "Never saw any of 'em before," he said.

"Then how will you know which ones are . . . who did you say? John and somebody?"

"John, he's the oldest. An' Albert, who was the third brother. Youngest now that Benjamin is dead."

"So how will you know them?"

Longarm grunted. "If they are the baddest of the bunch, I reckon I'll know them once I lay eyes on them. It's something a man knows, senses somehow. Don't know as I can explain it, but I'll know."

"I take your word for that, young man, and I am very glad that I do not really understand it."

"There," Longarm said. "There goes Miss Foster with a couple buckets o' food for the folks on that side o' the road. She's doin' what I said."

"She is a good woman. Dependable," Bennett said.

"Seems too good t' be a madam," Longarm said. "She looks like quality."

"She was." Bennett's voice was hesitant.

Longarm turned his head to look at the white-haired old cobbler. "You know something of her?"

Bennett nodded. "She comes from a good family. Good people but foolish. Her father is deeply in debt to Clete Thomas. Jessica is, you could say, working off her father's debt."

"Slavery," Longarm grunted. "It ain't stopped yet. Not with men like Thomas. Miss Foster. His own daughter Nelda. The man has been keeping them both as his slaves."

"Nelda is his daughter? I thought she was his mistress," Bennett blurted.

"Yeah," Longarm said. "Both o' them things."

"The man is slime, isn't he."

"And that is puttin' it mildly. Here comes Miss Foster, back for some more lunch buckets. An' . . . aw, hell. Here comes trouble."

Longarm picked up his purloined shotgun, the one poor Betsy had used when she tried to kill him, checked his pockets to make sure he had shells available in them, reflexively checked the Colt to assure himself that it slid free in its leather while the weight told him the revolver was fully loaded. He eared the shotgun hammers to full cock. That would save half a second if—when—it came to shooting.

He was about as ready as he could hope to be.

Now if only everyone else was . . .

Chapter 39

Longarm stepped out onto the boardwalk in front of Titus Bennett's shoe shop.

It was a fine day, one of those cool, high country days when the sky is so blue it fair hurts a man's eyes to look at it. Not so much as a wisp of cloud up there. Air so crystal clear you could practically taste it. The Cheyenne would call it a good day to die. Longarm considered it a good day to carry a badge and address the law. A good day indeed.

He took a child's tin whistle out of his pocket and blew into it, sending a shrill note that could be heard from one end of town to the other.

He neither heard nor saw any response. But then he was not supposed to. Neither was anyone else.

The five riders came down the road from Hartsel. Only five, he saw. Not as large a gang as he'd expected. Some must have dropped out. Drinking and whoring down in Colorado City perhaps or gone up to Denver for the many fleshpots to be found there.

It pleased him to see there were only five. Five might just be manageable.

"That's far enough," he announced when the riders reached a point ten yards or so from him.

He stepped down off the boardwalk and into the street, facing the gang with his feet slightly apart, the shotgun held in both hands, index finger resting lightly on the front trigger of the 12 gauge.

He looked them over. There was a smallish man—at least compared to the others in the bunch—riding on the left of the formation and slightly behind the others.

The man's position said he was a follower but the wolfish expression and cold eyes suggested this was the one who called the shots. This, Longarm believed, would be John Cranston.

Longarm examined each of the five, then returned to the leader. "You'd be John," he said.

The rider nodded slightly. He held his reins in his left hand. His right hung down close to his thigh. And close to the walnut grips of a revolver.

"I'm United States Deputy Marshal Custis Long."

There seemed to be a flicker of interest in the leader's eyes. "Heard of you, mister. You're the one they call Longarm, ain't you? Like in the long arm of the law."

"That's one way t' look at it," Longarm agreed. "There's others."

"We'd take it kindly, Long, if you would step aside an' leave us be about our business."

"I've already taken care o' the business you'll have in mind."

"How so?" John Cranston asked.

"I looked into your brother's death. He wasn't froze, he was murdered. I've caught the murderer an' I'll see that he hangs, legal an' proper after a trial before a judge, not in no street shoot-out. I've also had your brother's body exhumed an' put into a proper coffin. That coffin is settin' around back of that mercantile over there, already loaded onto a buckboard ready for you boys to carry with you wherever you want your kin buried."

"Now that's real nice o' you, Long, but you shouldn't of gone to the trouble. This is something we'll take care of our own selves. Now kindly step aside and leave us to it."

"Reckon not, boys." He looked up toward the roof tops, where of a sudden there were ten round, black objects showing, objects that looked for all the world like rifle or shotgun barrels.

One of the riders blanched at the sight. His nervousness transmitted to his horse and it began to tremble and curvet. The man had trouble trying to hold it in place. After a few seconds he gave up the effort, spun the animal around over its hocks, and lit out for far places just as fast as he could flog that horse into going.

"Shit," one of the Cranston boys shouted.

Longarm tripped the front trigger of his shotgun, sending a load of buck into John Cranston's belly.

Cranston was thrown backward from his saddle. His rearing horse got in the way of Longarm's second blast. The buckshot struck the animal in the side of the head and dropped it instantly.

Longarm palmed his Colt and put two quick rounds into the chest of the one he suspected would be Albert.

Before Louis or the remaining sidekick could get into the fight, they were looking down at dynamite bundles with smoky, sputtering fuses, tossed down from the roof-tops nearby.

The dynamite exploded practically underneath the bellies of the horses, unseating both riders.

Longarm was on them before either man could re-cover his wits. He slashed the backs of their heads with the barrels of the shotgun, knocking the sidekick out and putting a bloody dent in Louis Cranston's skull, too.

He was out of handcuffs so Longarm had to settle for tying the remaining two using the same twine he had used to make up his dynamite bundles.

By then the townspeople and the whores were com-ing down off the roofs. They looked awfully proud of themselves.

"How'd we do?" a man called Grenville asked.

"Clockwork," Longarm told him. "Couldn't o' been any better. You fellas haul these assholes over to where we have Clete an' Jim Tanzy stashed, will you? And you an' you, take care o' burying these men, will you? Better take Ben Cranston back to his grave, too. I don't reckon his brothers will be takin' him anywhere like I offered." He grinned and said, "You don't have t' be real gentle with these two neither."

"What about you?" another man asked.

"Me, I'm gonna take all the live ones up to Fairplay. I'll do that tomorrow mornin'. Seems a mite late t' be starting that trip this afternoon."

He looked at Jessica Foster and said, "This afternoon I'll be wanting t' get me some bed rest."

"I have a room you can use," the lovely redhead said.

The woman was no virgin, Longarm knew. Clete Thomas had had her as his slave. And Ben Cranston had had her as his lover. But there was much about the woman that he did not know.

He smiled.

This afternoon. Tonight. There would be time enough for Longarm to find out the things he wanted to know.

Watch for

LONGARM AND THE RUNAWAY NURSE

the 393rd novel in the exciting LONGARM
series from Jove

Coming in August!